Barnsley Libraries

P.S.2027

ROYSTON   2 2 JUL 2019
          - 3 MAR 2022
05/14

ROUNDHOUSE

22 DEC 14   1 7 FEB 2024

= MAY 2018   1 6 MAR 2024

2 3 JUL 2018   1 4 MAY 2024

2 3 AUG 2018
- 4 SEP 2018   1 5 AUG 2024

               2 4 OCT 2024

               - 3 JAN 2025

3805900559516 2

Trouble-Shooting Johnny

Johnny Rayno was tall, lean and strong. He was quite handsome too and, in keeping with his trade, he moved like a cat. Here, indeed, was a gunfighter offering his services to Ace-High Logan, the most powerful man in Fishknife Territory. No sooner had he been hired than he and the rest of the men from the Logan ranch were ambushed, with one man killed and another wounded. Thanks to Johnny the bushwhackers were routed.

This was only the beginning, though, and a full-scale range war quickly erupted. Hot lead was destined to fly and many would never live to see another day before, at long last, peace was finally restored and grim justice done.

Trouble-Shooting Johnny

Brad Shannon

A Black Horse Western

ROBERT HALE · LONDON

© 1958, 2003 Vic J. Hanson
First hardcover edition 2003
Originally published in paperback as
Trouble Shooting Johnny by Vern Hanson

ISBN 0 7090 7269 4

Robert Hale Limited
Clerkenwell House
Clerkenwell Green
London EC1R OHT

The right of Vic J. Hanson to be identified as
author of this work has been asserted by him
in accordance with the Copyright, Designs and
Patents Act 1988.

Typeset by
Derek Doyle & Associates, Liverpool.
Printed and bound in Great Britain by
Antony Rowe Limited, Wiltshire

CHAPTER I

He stepped from the shaded sidewalk into the glare of the sun on the main drag. It was very hot. But, as she watched him from the window, Amy shivered a little. The first thing she had noticed was the way he carried himself. Like a cat; but far from jumpy. And, as he came nearer, the other things fell into place. She had seen so many like him. Seen them advancing catlike through gunsmoke. Seen a few of them go down too. Young men, supple men, devil-may-care men, laughter on their lips and death in their eyes.

This one was tall and lean and young. Quite handsome too, a broken nose giving him an attractively rakish appearance.

The dress didn't matter. Shabby cowhands' clothes, rundown high-heeled riding-boots, chaps. The guns were the things you noticed! This one wore two of them, the holsters tied to his thighs by whang-strings. His hands almost brushed those holsters as he walked.

As if suddenly aware of her gaze, he looked up. She

dodged back behind the curtain. She thought probably he had caught a glimpse of her. But then, almost at once, he was out of her sight and she knew he had passed on through the door of the hotel. Her father would be awaiting him down there in the lounge, seated there at the big round table in the corner: the king with his courtiers around him.

She went and sat on the edge of the bed. She had done all her shopping in the town that morning. There was nothing else to see, nothing else to do. She just had to wait until her father was ready to leave. Would the stranger be going back to the ranch with them, she wondered?

She had liked the look of him. But, if he did come back to the ranch wouldn't it prove he was just like all the rest, ready to sell his gun to the highest bidder? And nobody in Fishknife Territory could afford to bid any higher than her father. Little wonder they called him Ace-High Logan.

Right then (she visualised the scene) old Ace-High was introducing the stranger to his courtiers. Joe Keene, Darkie Boots; Sam Joubert, Rafe Dawson. A pretty quartet. And the stranger, who seemed oblivious of the eyes boring into him as he straddled a chair, called himself Johnny Rayno.

It is quite probable that Amy Logan, despite her extensive nodding aquaintance with gunmen had never heard of Johnny Rayno. But the five men at the round table had.

Ace-High asked Rayno how much he wanted. Rayno

told them. Then Joe Keene, the ramrod, said:

'You put a big price on yourself, young fellah.'

Ace-High glared at Joe for speaking out of turn. AceHigh said: 'I'll pay it. But I'll expect you to earn it. Yuh ready to start?'

'I'm ready!' said Johnny Rayno.

'We'll go out to the ranch right away.' Ace-High turned his head. 'Darkie, go tell Miss Amy.'

So the half-caste ranny fetched Amy and she was introduced to Johnny Rayno and the whole bunch of them set out for the ranch.

Johnny Rayno saw a yellow-haired girl with a good shape, pouting red lips and eyes blue as prairie cornflowers. She strode her horse like she had grown in the saddle. She rode at the head of the group, next to her father, imperious princess beside her king. After the initial introduction she ignored Johnny. Or so he thought.

She noticed that his nose was indeed broken and wondered how that had come to pass. His hair was raven-black and he wore it fashionably long. He wasn't much older than herself, she figured. Twenty-five or twenty-six maybe.

Old Ace-High was jealous of his daughter's prestige. He had probably never heard the word 'snob' – but snob he was. Consequently, Amy had become mistress of the art of the sidelong glance. She had eyelashes admirably constructed for this: long and black and silky in contrast to her coarse sun-bleached yellow hair.

But after a time, she got tired of trying to weigh Johnny Rayno up and did indeed ignore him. She had decided he would serve to break the monotony around the ranch. But, after all, wasn't he like the rest of them, here to kill or be killed? His face now had a set look, withdrawn. But his mouth was mobile and there were grin-wrinkles at the corner of his eyes. He didn't look like a killer.

A sleek black cat seldom looked like a killer – but invariably was.

The bunch, their business transacted, rode in silence. They reached the bluffs which were approximately halfway between the town of Fishknife and the Logan ranch. The narrow trail bent sharply here, rounded the bluffs.

The small cavalcade rounded the first bluff. Then things began to happen.

Shooting started up from the rocks around them. Ace-High's hat was whisked from his head. The shock made him reel in the saddle and, with a startled cry Amy grabbed for him. And, as if to echo her cry, came another, more horrible one from close behind her. Joe Keene, the ramrod, hit the ground and rolled, screaming, his hands wrapped across his middle.

Ace-High's horse bolted, the old man rocking in the saddle, his iron-grey hair in disarray. Amy spurred her mount after them. Her sombrero, held by a leather string, bobbed on her shoulders. Her yellow hair streamed in the wind. Oblivious of the carnage behind her she was anxious only for her father.

Darkie Boots, Sam Joubert, Rafe Dawson and Johnny Rayno scattered for cover on the other side of the trail. Joe Keene had stopped squirming and yelling. He was dead.

Darkie Boots was cursing in two languages as he tried to stanch the blood from a flesh-wound in his shoulder. The dandified Sam Joubert had a heel shot neatly from one of his riding-boots. He had been mighty proud of those boots. Rafe Dawson was unscathed and had managed to take his deadly little sawn-off shotgun into cover with him. Johnny Rayno had left his hat behind him on the trail. He brushed strays of black hair away from his eyes with his elbow. His hands were full of hardware.

Two other horses, besides the one ridden by Ace-High had bolted. Another one lay dead. Only Johnny's spavined-looking grey colt had sought cover and was now browsing in the grass yards behind his master.

Johnny dug himself in as a slug almost took his ear off. Glancing around, he saw that by now his new comrades were firmly entrenched too. The bushwhackers had been over-eager: instead of picking their men they had obviously blazed away indiscriminately as soon as the small cavalcade came into view round the bend.

He didn't know how many there were on the other side: they were too well-hidden. He didn't know who they were. Just the enemy. He was back fighting the enemy again. Any enemy. He fell back into the familiar pattern of things. This was the kind of shindig for which he had been trained through the years . . . as a camp-boy with Quantrell's Raiders, as a deputy-marshal in border hell-holes, as a troubleshooter all over the old South West – and on the other side of the border too.

The enemy set up another barrage and under cover of it, keeping his head well down, he began to crawl. He was taking a big chance but he had been taking the same kind of chances for most of his life. It had never been his practice to make like a turkey at a shoot for assorted snipers.

A slug chipped the heel of his boot, another plucked at the sleeve of his shirt. Slugs smacked into rock, ricocheted, whined away into the sun-haze. In a slight lull Johnny heard Sam Joubert scream out a rebel yell. The dapper ranny sounded a mite hysterical. The Ace-High boys were retaliating in strength now. Johnny reached the end of the rock outcrop. The width of the narrow trail still lay between him and the foe. To try and cross that would be sheer suicide. But he had accomplished one thing by his manoeuvre. Unnoticed, he had partially outflanked the other bunch. He could see one of them very clearly and had glimpses of two or three more.

The nearest bushwhacker was a big fellow with hanks of long red hair escaping from beneath his battered Stetson. He was oblivious of Johnny. Lips drawn back from teeth in a killer-snarl, he was pumping lead at the three men entrenched on the other side of the trail.

Johnny glanced down the trail. Ace-High Logan and his daughter were no longer to be seen. Johnny hefted his guns, feeling the smooth weight of them, the balls of his thumbs resting gently on the hammers above the filed-down hair-triggers.

There was another lull in the shooting and he rose a little and opened his mouth wide and yelled. A hideous ear-splitting yell that galvanized its hearers. The redheaded man whirled and Johnny saw his staring eyes, his mouth yammering. Then the killer-snarl was back on the beefy face and the gun was lifted, the barrel thrown down on Johnny.

Johnny started shooting, the guns bucking and flaming in his hands, his blood singing with a wild exultation. The red-headed man went down like a dummy at a County Fair. The man behind him spun around like a crazy top, his hands flapping a signal to the skies. He went down too.

Men were showing themselves now at both sides of the trail. As if released by Johnny's crazy yell, a reckless fury seemed to have taken hold of everybody.

But it soon passed and the smoke and dust cleared and the bushwhackers took to their horses. The four Ace-High men had only one horse between them, so they couldn't very well give chase. So they crossed the trail and discovered they had downed three of the other side. All three of them were dead. Sam Joubert sang out their names, which meant nothing to Johnny. But Darkie and Rafe didn't evince any surprise at Sam's revelations.

'Leave 'em,' said Sam. 'We best go after the boss an' Amy. The ol' man might've been hit.'

'What do we do for horses?' growled Rafe Dawson.

He was stocky and powerfully-built with a pug face. He looked like an ex-prizefighter. He carried the shortest sawn-off shotgun Johnny had ever seen, a wicked-looking little weapon. He had definitely put paid to one of the bushwhackers, cutting him almost in half with a hail of smallshot.

'I don't expect they've gone far,' said Darkie Boots in his deep voice.

He was obviously a mulatto, and a very handsome one, a man of about Johnny's own age, rangy and muscular, fast-looking. Johnny went and collected his own horse and they put the body of Joe Keene across the saddle. The four men set off, walking a little awkwardly on their high-heeled riding-boots. Johnny led his mount.

Pretty soon, however, they came on the other three horses, grazing quietly. They mounted. A little further on they met another party from the Ace-High spread. The old man and Amy had gotten home safely and had sent reinforcements out. Johnny was introduced all round. He decided these boys were a pretty hard bunch – and he'd seen some in his time. He noticed that there were no extravagant signs of grief shown at the demise of Joe Keene. Evidently Joe hadn't been a particularly popular ramrod.

CHAPTER II

They reached the ranch, an imposing sight in the small valley bathed by sunshine. Sam Joubert left the rest. Johnny watched the dapper cowhand walk to the large white-painted ranch house with the verandah and the flower gardens.

'I guess Sam'll get to be ramrod now,' said Darkie Boots.

The mulatto boy's surmise proved to be correct. Johnny was called to the ranch house a little later. The old man commended Rayno on his shooting prowess: evidently Sam Joubert had spoken well of the new man. Yeah, from now on everybody was to take orders from Sam. Any questions, asked the old man. Johnny Rayno said no; and, even as he did so, men were digging a grave out beyond the corral to take the remains of Joe Keene.

This wealthy pleasant-looking spread was used to sudden death. There was menace beneath the white paint and the flowers under the hot sun.

Johnny didn't see Amy Logan around, so he asked

Ace-High if the girl was all right. The old man looked at him sharply. 'She's fine,' he said. He jerked his leonine grey head in the curt gesture of dismissal. Johnny went.

The reception to Sam Joubert's promotion was mixed. In the first few days Sam went out of his way to be nice to everybody. Ordinary times he was a fairly likeable cuss but Johnny learned that when he lost his temper Sam was a hysterical savage. But a little time was to elapse before the new man was to see a really prime example of this side of the ramrod's character.

And all the time he was learning plenty about the set-up in Fishknife territory.

The Ace-High ranch was by far the biggest in the territory. In fact, until recent years it had been *the* spread and old Ace-High was literally monarch of all he surveyed and a heck of a lot more besides that too. Ace-High's only rival had been Jasper Kane, who ran the C Gauntlet ranch on the other side of the creek known as Old Slowcoach.

Old Slowcoach had been the dividing line between the two ranches and their owners, friends since boyhood, had managed to rub along pretty evenly. Then, quite suddenly, Jasper Kane died and his widow, an Eastern filly much younger than old Jasper, sold the spread, lock stock and barrel, to an Eastern combine and went back East herself.

The combine let the range out to smallholders, no less than eleven families of them all told. Many of these 'sodbusters' were not even Texans, but came from as far away as Kansas. They used the creek for all kinds of purposes and fouled it up considerably. And when, in the hot season, Old Slowcoach was dried up in parts, they ran their stock on Ace-High land. That much of the stock was hated sheep, which ate up the fine grass like a swarm of locusts, was the crowning humiliation.

So the Ace-High got rough. And the nesters banded together and retaliated. Fishknife territory simmered on the edge of a range-war.

Johnny Rayno couldn't help thinking that, even if he wasn't employed by the Ace-High he'd be inclined to be on their side. A Texan himself, he had been raised in the wide cattle country. Hatred of nesters and, above all, nesters who brought 'woolies' to ravage the grasslands, was inherent in him.

He wasn't quite sure yet just exactly where he fitted in the set-up but he figured he'd soon find out. In the meantime he did a top-hand's job as good as the next man.

The ambush-party he had helped to scatter on his welcome to Fishknife territory had been composed solely of nesters. Joe Keene had died. Three nesters had died. The sheriff had come out from town to see the old man. Johnny, who had been out on the range at the time, hadn't even got to see the lawman. Not that he had any particular interest in lawmen – though he had more than once acted as one himself. There was no more action for a while. The sheriff had probably paid a visit to the leaders of the nester factions too. Old Ace-

High, a law unto himself, found it expedient to pay lip-service to the law from time to time. Evidently the other side could play at that game too.

There was one small incident. An Ace-High line-hut was burned to the ground in the absence of the two riders who bivouacked there. They hadn't seen a soul – so it could have been an accident. And, like men's hates, the range simmered in the hot sun. And there was a tense waiting atmosphere in the air that began to get on men's nerves.

A horse-race was fixed to break the monotony. Johnny Rayno entered his own spavined-looking grey colt and thus brought the scorn of the rest of the bunch down upon his head.

'I'm willing to back him with hard cash,' grinned the new man.

He was taken up on this by everybody in sight, all the riders in fact who were not on duty at that particular time.

Seven riders lined up, Johnny Rayno among them. Darkie Boots was another. Sam Joubert, who had elected to be starter, stood with his gun lifted. Then Darkie's horse, a wicked-looking brown stallion, elected to throw a fit of temperament.

Maybe to him the lifted gun held by Sam was a threat. He broke ranks and reared. Sam stepped backwards just in time. The ironshod hoofs missed him by inches. He lost his balance and fell on his back, his legs in the air. His gun landed in the dust beside him.

Darkie quietened his fractious mount. A few of the men laughed. But the laughter died as, slowly, Sam Joubert rose. His face was suffused with blood; his eyes were crazy. He grabbed the gun, levelled it at Darkie.

'Goddam you! You! . . . you did that on purpose . . .'

His voice was strangled, his words lapsed into incoherency.

Darkie was unarmed. All the race-riders had, before mounting, taken off their gunbelts and hung them over the corral rails.

Darkie said, 'Honest, Sam I. . . .'

Then he stopped, an incredulous expression on his dark, handsome face. It all happened so quickly. The movements, the words, the action . . . Johnny Rayno, who was nearest, kicked the gun out of Sam's hand.

'Man! You shouldn't shoot him for that. . . .'

Sam turned his savage hate-filled gaze on Johnny. But he did not make another move for the gun in the dust.

Darkie said, 'He meant to do it all right. It was 'cos the fellas laughed at him. He's like to go crazy when he's roused.' Then, as if the full enormity of Sam's intention suddenly came to him, his voice rose, 'But I'll take him if he still wants it. I'll take him. . . .'

But Sam Joubert spun on his heels and moved towards the bunkhouse.

Darkie said, 'He ain't gonna forgive either of us for this, Johnny. Thanks an' all – if you hadn't acted so fast he'd've plugged me for shore.'

Johnny shook his head slowly from side to side, as if

he still couldn't believe it. 'I couldn't just sit there, Darkie,' he said. 'I was glad to do it.'

'Imagine having a loco man like that one for a foreman,' said another of the men disgustedly.

One of the spectators picked up Sam's gun and placed it near the others at the corral rails. Sam had vanished into the bunkhouse. He did not reappear. So, after a bit, the race was run and Johnny astonished everybody by winning it on his freak-looking horse. He collected in the dinero, divulging then that privately he called his horse Lightnin'.

When the boys got back to the bunkhouse, Sam Joubert was no longer around. One of the men said sneeringly that maybe 'Fancy-pants' (as he called him) had gone carrying tales to the old man. Evidently the rank and file had little respect for their new ramrod; and this latest incident hadn't strengthened it any.

Sam didn't turn up for chow either and the cook said he had seen the ramrod ride out in the direction of town.

Men left just after that to relieve the night-herders. The rest, Johnny and Darkie among them, prepared to hit the hay.

After the usual smoke and exchange of gossip and tall stories the hurricane-lamp was blown out and there was a running chorus of 'good-nights'.

'Maybe some o' them pesky nesters caught ol' Sam,' said a man drowzily.

Only snores answered him.

A little later, however, the sound of hammering hoofs

awakened almost everybody. Then the bunkhouse door was flung open and guns were grabbed.

'Light the lamp somebody,' said the hoarse breathless voice of Sam Joubert.

Somebody did so. Sam blinked in the yellow rays. He was dishevelled. His face looked like a horse had trampled on it. Everybody watched him as he undressed but nobody spoke.

He had his pants off when the door was flung open again. Old Ace-High stood there.

His eyes stabbed around the room, rested on Sam, the only one out of bed.

'Was that you who just rode in, in such a flaming hurry?'

'Yes. I . . .'

'Get something on an' come back to the ranch house. I want to talk to you.' The door slammed behind the old man.

Sam didn't look at anybody. He dressed himself again, everything except his gunbelt; he left the place.

He was away an hour or more. He didn't ask for the light this time but undressed in the dark.

Early next morning a posse came and took him away. The old man wasn't to be seen. A little later the cook was able to tell the whole story.

He cooked at the ranch house too. He had been doing the breakfast when the law arrived. He'd heard everything.

Sam Joubert had gotten roaring drunk in town, had gotten in a fight with a couple of nesters; not members of the rough company but pretty inoffensive Kansas farm boys by all accounts. Sam had stunned one of them with a chair, but the other one had taken over and given Sam a beating, all fair and square.

Half-an-hour later the kid was found in an alley with a bullet in his back. Sam was caught in the vicinity. One shot had been fired from his gun.

That was the tale the sheriff had told Ace-High. Possemen had backed it up. The old man sent for Sam. Sam admitted the fight, said he'd been mean-drunk. But he hadn't shot the kid in the back. He was good with his gun – he didn't have to go around shooting folks in the back.

He couldn't fight the posse. They disarmed him. The old man couldn't do a thing and, the cook said, didn't seem as if he wanted to.

Among the men, opinions were divided. Some said Sam was crazy enough for anything, he'd done the job all right. Others said, Sam might be wild but he had more savvy than to shoot a man in the back, particularly when he stood fair to be the first one suspected. Besides, like the cook reported Sam having said himself, he was fast with a gun: he could've picked a fight with the Kansas boy later, forced him to draw, got him that way, plenty of witnesses to cry 'self defence'. It had been done plenty times before, they affirmed cynically.

On the other hand, most of them had to admit that when Sam was in a rage he didn't seem responsible for his own actions.

Nobody else had yet been promoted to ramrod in Sam's place. Old Ace-High stayed in the white house like an old eagle in his eyrie. His daughter, Amy, wasn't seen around much either. Rafe Dawson acted as liaison officer between the ranch house and the boys in the bunkhouse. One of the orders that came through was that the men should stay away from town. Work went on as usual. The Ace-High men were picked cowhands: they didn't have to be continually told what to do.

Another day passed. No news came through from town. Rafe Dawson said the old man hadn't even mentioned Sam Joubert.

CHAPTER III

Another broiling hot day. The men worked off their tension in the late afternoon by indulging in target-practice behind the bunkhouse.

There was a dilapidated fence there, all that remained of what had once been a chicken-run, an incongruous thing to find around a cattle-ranch. Chickens had been kept here years ago by the cook's wife, a bundle of stringy female dynamite called Lucillinda. Everybody, including Cookie had been mighty relieved when this virago took up with a passing drummer selling hardware and lit out for pastures new. She hadn't been heard of since. The hands, slowly forgetting her, became bold and ate off the chickens. Nobody bothered to replace them.

The dilapidated fence, still known jocularly as the birdcorral, was ideal for target-practice. Cans and bottles were balanced along its rails. Playing cards, horseshoe nails and busted dimes were driven into its posts. It was pitted with bullet-holes, eaten away in places. The ground around it was littered with relics testifying to the exuberance of a long line of Ace-High pistolers.

Darkie Boots and Rafe Dawson were among the sharpshooting merchants who tested their prowess on that particular hot afternoon. Johnny Rayno and others of the men stood on the sidelines watching.

The shimmering heat-haze and the dust made shooting difficult. But both Darkie and Rafe were giving a good account of themselves. For shooting ability there wasn't a pin to put between them. They shot the necks neatly from bottles. They made cans do crazy parabolas in the air with singing lead. They drilled coins, split them in half. They shot the pips from playing-cards.

Then, during a lull while they wiped sweat from their brows Rafe turned on Johnny Rayno and said:

'C'mon, gunslinger. Don't just stand there. Let's see what you can do.'

Men stared, wondering how Rayno would take this rather blustering challenge. But the new man just grinned.

He was indolent, his legs crossed so that it seemed he might overbalance at any minute. Then suddenly he moved, his feet going slap-slap in the dust. His guns were in his hands then; two shots blended into a single crashing report.

A can was driven from the ground, lifted by the two slugs. Another slug chipped it, sent it higher, started it spinning. Johnny kept it spinning till he had emptied his guns. Then he let it fall.

'Yeah, man . . . yeah,' sang out Darkie Boots. 'That's what 'a call real shooting.'

Rafe Dawson looked a little disgruntled, but he managed to say, 'Shore thing.'

There was a spatter of clapping. Johnny reloaded his guns. Other contestants began to join in. The air vibrated with gunfire.

Old Ace-High put in an appearance and stood and watched. He loved good shooting. Then Cookie hammered his triangle and called 'Come an' git it' and the men began to drift away in the direction of the cook-shack.

As Johnny Rayno was passing him, Ace-High said, 'When you've had your meal come to the ranch house.'

'Sure, boss,' said the new man.

Ace-High was working in his study. Sometimes he hollered for black coffee and it was Amy's practice to make it for him, rather than bother Cookie in his den with such a small chore. The nights were getting longer in the tooth. The heat was oppressive but everybody knew it would break soon and there would be rain. Ace-High, more peevish than usual, had refused his tea, had shut himself up with his books and papers, squatting like some craggy primeval cave-man among his guns, his pipes, his memories of his beautiful dead wife and the dawn of the Frontier which he had helped to build.

Amy tapped the door and, at the old man's grunt, opened it, went in. 'How about some coffee and cookies, Dad?'

'All right. And if that young fellah comes, show him right in here.'

'What young fellow?'

'The new man – Rayno.'

'Yes, all right.'

Why was Ace-High seeing the young gunfighter in private, Amy wondered. What were those two cooking up between them?

She took her father's tray in. He didn't look up from his papers, merely grunted. Amy went back to the kitchen. She had saved some coffee for herself. Maybe Mr. Johnny Rayno would take a cup with her, she reflected. She was still wondering what was behind the new man's expected visit.

Well, maybe she would try and find out.

She took off her apron, ran her hands over her shirtwaist and tight brown skirt. She looked at herself in the mirror. She pushed back a stray lock of golden hair, ran her hand gently down her face. Her lips were full and red, her eyes bright. She undid the top button of her shirtwaist, telling herself it was too hot for her to keep buttoned up like that.

She looked down at her small feet, clad in bright beaded moccasins. Her bare tanned legs had a good shape.

A rap on the door startled her. She hadn't heard a sound before this. The visitor must have moved like a cat. She opened the door.

Johnny Rayno took off his hat. 'Evenin', ma'am.'

'Good evening. Come in will you. My father is waiting for you in his study. I will show you where it is.'

She led the way, knowing her figure and carriage were good, that she made a pretty picture. She knocked her father's door, called, 'Mr Rayno is here.'

'Send him in.'

She opened the door, ushered Johnny inside, left the two men together.

Her hand had touched Johnny's arm lightly as he passed her; he had been acutely aware of it. He wondered if it had been done purposely. He had not lived twenty-seven years odd without learning that he was attractive to women. From the age of fifteen or sixteen – and he was a damnsight prettier before he got his nose busted – female creatures had chased him, though not a one had yet succeeded in getting him hogtied.

But nothing of his thoughts showed in his face as he confronted the old man. He was as impassive as an Indian before Ace-High's eagle gaze.

'Sit down, son.'

Johnny sat on the hard chair on the opposite side of the desk, and Ace-High went on talking in his usual forthright manner.

'My old friend, Jim Capes down in the Pecos gave you a good build-up, Johnny. He said you were the best troubleshooter in Texas.'

'Jim Capes is a fine man,' said Johnny Rayno. 'I enjoyed working for him.'

'Why leave him then?'

The young man shrugged. 'I guess I'm just a natural fiddle-feet.'

'Did you get in trouble down there?'

'No more'n usual. If you mean is the law after me, the answer's No.'

'What's your opinion of Sam Joubert?'

'Don't know him well enough to say. A little wild I guess – but I don't claim to be no puff-ball myself.'

'No, but Sam's in jail and you're not. So I'm offering you the job of ramrod of this ranch. I think you can handle it. Do you?'

'Yes, suh. But some of the men ain't gonna like it.'

Ace-High half-rose. 'The men'll do as I say,' he boomed. 'You takin' the job or not?'

'I'll take the job, suh. Thank you.' But Johnny's dark poker face didn't change expression.

The old man smiled thinly. 'I'll leave you to tell the men the news yourself.'

The young man's eyes kindled a little but his face did not change. 'Yes, suh,' he said and rose.

The old man abruptly thrust forth his hand. They shook.

'Good-night, Johnny.'

'Good-night, suh.'

As the new foreman made his way down the passage Amy appeared in the doorway of the kitchen. He was almost touching her when she swiftly stepped aside.

'Will you take a cup of fresh coffee with me, Mr Rayno?'

For an infinitismal moment he hesitated; then he said, 'I'll be mighty glad to, ma'am. Thank you.'

'Don't call me ma'am,' she said. 'It makes me feel old.

Call me Amy. But when dad's around don't forget to call me *Miss* Amy. Dad's a stickler for the proprieties.'

Johnny smiled. 'You scared of your old man?'

'I am not. It's just that . . .' She gave a little shrug, turned away from him, busied herself at the stove. 'Sit down,' she said over her shoulder.

He seated himself at the table. She brought two cups of coffee across, a plate of cookies.

She waited a while before asking softly, 'And what is the secret?'

Johnny swallowed a last mouthful of cookie. 'What secret?'

'The one between you and my father.'

'No secret. He just made me his foreman that's all.'

'Did that surprise you?'

'Some.'

'Why did he do it, do you think?'

'I guess he figured I was the man for the job.'

'Do you agree with him?'

He rose. 'I'll let you know – Amy. Thanks for the coffee and cookies. Mighty fine.'

She followed him to the door. He turned and she was close to him. He kissed her. One moment he was there; the next the night had swallowed him, leaving only the swiftness and warmth of him behind. Amy wanted to slap his face. But she knew if she did, that face's sombre darkness would only break into an impudent smile. And after a while she didn't really want to slap it at all, only to see it again.

CHAPTER IV

The attitude of the men towards the new ramrod was not particularly encouraging. Only Darkie Boots and Cookie openly congratulated him. The news hit Rafe Dawson the hardest. He had evidently fancied himself as the new foreman. He didn't speak a word to Johnny Rayno, but his black looks spoke volumes.

Things came to a head suddenly on the following night.

A rider had brought the news that a couple of days from now Sam Joubert was to be brought up for trial at the county seat, which was at Craneville seventy miles away.

'The sheriff and a couple of deputies are taking Sam,' went on the messenger. 'But the nesters are talking big – they say Sam will never reach the county seat.'

'I guess they could stop him at that,' said another of the company in the lighted bunkhouse.

'Unless we stop them first,' said a third man.

'That's it,' burst out Rafe Dawson. 'We've got to get

Sam out o' that jail, pronto. Tonight – tonight's the time, they won't be expecting us tonight.'

'Wait a minute,' said the voice of Johnny Rayno. 'Let's not go off half-cocked.'

Rafe Dawson whirled on him. The stocky red-haired man forgot he wasn't on speaking terms with the new ramrod. All his disappointment and hate came out in his voice as he snarled:

'No, you wouldn't want Sam back here, would you, Rayno?'

Johnny ignored the insulting questions. He said: 'The old man wouldn't want it like this. Let it ride a bit. Sam's still got another twenty-four hours or so. Maybe the old man's got something up his sleeve. Something legal that'll get Sam free without any bloodshed.'

'The old man needn't know,' said one man.

'If you ask me the old man's already given Sam up to the wolves,' said another.

It seemed as if these men who, only the day before, had dismissed Sam as a trigger-happy cuss full of loco weed, were now right behind him. In any case, they were on the side of Rafe Dawson and Rafe was quick to seize upon this. His voice rang out again.

'It suits Mr Rayno for Sam to rot in jail or be lynched by the nesters. If Sam comes back here maybe Mr Rayno will lose his nice new job.'

Then Johnny had stood enough. 'You'll take that back, Dawson,' he said.

Men began to move aside, leaving these two a

cleared space. They had both just come in off the range, they both wore their guns.

'You'll make me take it back!' said Rafe Dawson. 'You'll make me.' His face was suffused with blood. He fell into a crouch.

'Don't be a fool, Rafe,' said Darkie Boots softly. 'You wouldn't have a chance.'

'I don't aim to kill a good top-hand,' said Johnny Rayno. 'Take your belt off, Rafe.'

Slowly Rafe's flush died. He unbuckled his gun-belt, handed it to a man behind him. Darkie took Johnny's gear and, as soon as the ramrod's hands were empty Rafe charged.

His right fist caught Johnny on the side of the head, spinning him around. But Rafe was a little precipitate: his follow-up blow only grazed Johnny's shoulder and Rafe, boring forward, was off-balance, giving Johnny time to orient himself. He spun, slamming a blow at Rafe, catching him on the chin. Rafe went backwards. A few of the watchers scattered. Johnny pulled off, looked around him, knowing that more than one man here was quite capable of putting a knife in his back.

He knew he had his hands full with Rafe without somebody else taking a hand. What Rafe lost in height and reach he made up for in weight and strength. He was built like a pint-size grizzly-bear.

Rafe bored in again, using his knee this time. He was past-master at the gentle art of the rough-house – and nothing barred. Johnny took the burrowing knee on his thigh. It punished him but did not move him; he slammed two blows to Rafe's middle, heard the stocky man gasp, saw him bend a little. His elbow swept round in a neat follow-up, cracked against the side of Rafe's jaw. But Rafe was already swinging wildly in retaliation: his blow caught Johnny in the chest, spinning him away.

Johnny almost skittled another man who hadn't tried to get out of the way soon enough. The fellah went for his gun.

Darkie Boots said softly, 'Don't try it, George, or I'll blow a hole right through you.'

The man froze. Darkie was mighty fast and he had an Indian-like implacability. Not missing this by-play and resolving to thank Darkie later, Johnny Rayno launched himself back once more at his opponent.

Rafe met him squarely in the centre of the floor and they tangled like two fighting roosters. This time the table got in the way. Rafe sprawled across it, Johnny on top of him. Locked together, they rolled. They finished up on the floor, scrabbling and spitting like a couple of wildcats.

When they got up they were still holding on to each other. Rafe's thumb gouged at Johnny's eye, missed its mark, drew a red streak down the younker's face.

Johnny's lips drew back from white teeth. He grabbed Rafe by the throat with both hands and shook him the way a terrier shakes a rat. The bunch of watchers roared and stamped, too excited now to take sides.

Rafe used his knees, his nails, his elbows and finally

broke that cruel grip. He stabbed with his heel at Johnny's knee-cap. The ramrod hissed with pain. But he seemed to fight the pain off; he threw a right hand at Rafe with all he'd got. It caught the red-headed ranny smack on the point, shooting him across the room and putting him on his back beneath a bunk. He lay still.

That last blow had been the finisher. 'Nice work, Johnny,' said Darkie and gave the ramrod his gun-belt back.

Johnny strapped his guns on, tied the whang-strings around his flanks. It had been a purely mechanical act; but now he wondered whether he would have a use for his guns tonight.

The temper of the bunch had changed a little. The new ramrod had proved he could use his fists as well as his guns. Rafe Dawson was dragged from beneath the bunk and Cookie brought forth a bowl of water which was thrown over the prostrate man. Rafe came to, spluttering. He was helped to his feet. His eyes roved around the room until they found Johnny Rayno. Then Rafe strode forward and held out his hand.

'You beat me fair an' square, boss. I gotta hand it to yuh.'

Johnny watched the red-headed man warily. But he took the hand, shook it.

'I'll go see what the old man has to say about this new slant on Sam Joubert,' he said.

Darkie Boots said, 'You best go clean up first. You look like you been through a thresher.'

Looking at Rafe Dawson's blood-streaked face, Johnny realized his own must be pretty much the same.

Johnny went into the kitchen. Rafe followed him.

They didn't speak during their ablutions. Johnny went on to the ranch house.

Ace-High said pretty much what Johnny had figured he would.

'We can't buck the law with bullets this time, son. The case looks pretty black for Sam. But no nesters are gonna take the law into their own hands if I can help it. We've got a little more time. We'll wait and see. Let me know if anything turns up.'

'Sure. Goodnight, suh.'

'Goodnight, Johnny.'

The new ramrod left the place. He was peeved that he had not even caught a glimpse of Amy. Was she deliberately avoiding him?

But Amy, who had been doing some chores upstairs, was peeved too when she heard Johnny had been a-visiting. She hadn't seen him since last night. It had seemed a long time.

The hot night carried the stink of sheep. And on the other side of Old Slowcoach, Jubel Maxwell the nester leader gathered his captains about him.

They sat in the parlour of the four-roomed cabin in which Jubel lived with his wife, his son and his daughter. Jubel was the biggest sheepman in Fishknife Territory but, even so, his spread could've been stuck in one corner of Ace-High Logan's holdings on the other side of the creek and never noticed.

Jubel was a tall lean character with a hatchet face, unusually pale for an outdoor man, and dark deepset eyes. He always wore black storeclothes and old-fashioned knee-high riding boots. He looked like one of those fanatical travelling gospel-shouters that descended on the West from time to time.

Preacher he was not. But fanatic he certainly was!

He hated the arrogant Ace-High Logan (another fanatic!) and all he stood for with a hatred that at times shook him like a storm.

But he was calm now, calculating, as he spoke to the three other men at the table with him.

'The boys have done their work well. They've bragged their heads off. The word has been spread around town that Sam Joubert will never reach the county seat. It's taken for granted of course that we'll jump the law-party with Joubert someplace out on the trail. Word's bound to get to old Ace-High and I can't see the ol' buzzard letting one of his men, guilty or not, be taken by us.

'He'll probably plant scouts out on the trail. Or even try to get Joubert away beforehand. So that's where we'll fool both him and the law. We're going to raid that jail tonight, just the four of us. We'll have that skunk kicking at the end of a rope before anybody even knows he's gone. An' if we work things carefully nobody'll be able to prove who took him.'

The door opened and a little one-eyed hunchback came in.

Jubel whirled. 'F'r Pete's sake, Loopy, how many times have I gotta tell yuh not to bust in here without knockin'.'

'I'm sorry, Mistuh Maxwell,' bleated the man. 'I just thought mebbe you gents might like some cawfee.'

'We've got whiskey. What would we want with coffee? Go to bed.' Jubel's voice was harsh and the little hunchbacked odd-job man wilted before it the way he always did. He backed out, shut the door.

But he did not go to his bed, if a straw pallet in a stinking barn could be called a bed. No, he led his flea-bitten nag, his only possession away from the house where Jubel and his friends plotted and the family slept.

Not till Loopy was out of earshot did he awkwardly mount the horse. Then he rode like the wind.

They called him Loopy because he was deformed and he only had one eye and his nerves, like his body, had been shredded by blast-shock during the war between the States. He was an Easterner, representative of all the 'damn Yankees' a fanatical Reb like Jubel Maxwell was bound to hate. And Jubel never ceased to rub Loopy Kenwood's face in the dirt. But the little hunchback, when his shattered nerves were not playing him tricks was far from as loopy as he seemed. And already he had half-committed himself secretly to a new boss, a boss who, though ruthless, at least treated Loopy like a human being.

He did not slow his horse until he was approaching the Ace-High ranch buildings and then only because he knew the Ace-High boys were quick on the trigger and shot straight. He was challenged and he gave his name and asked to see the boss.

And, not for the first time, although he had retired old Ace-High got up to meet the spy from the other camp.

Loopy was a richer man when, half an hour later he left. Then Ace-High bawled for Johnny Rayno and, a little later still, Johnny woke some of the boys. Rafe Dawson, Darkie Boots and three others. The old man himself, despite his daughter's protests led them out.

The night was very dark. There was no wind and the heat was oppressive. White lights flashed now and then in the sky, reflections of a storm in the distance. The grass was parched and brittle for want of rain, the ground cracked. Old Slowcoach was dried up and already sheep were crossing its bed and straying on to Ace-High land. And this was just another score the old rancher had to settle with that sidewinder Maxwell and his bunch of sodbusters and woolly-chasers.

The bunch made a wide circuit of the town and went in over Boot Hill, through what was known as the back way. This led on to the commercial quarter of town and the offices, warehouses and suchlike were locked and dark.

They left their horses in a convenient alley near the jail. They moved along the backs of dark buildings, picking their way gingerly around ashcans, privies, piles of refuse, brokendown fences. From the back the jail was a high building, it needed no painted false walls to make it seem that way. The cell-block was at the back and could be distinguished by the row of small barred windows very high in the adobe wall. Everything was dark and silent.

'We can't get at him that way,' said Ace-High. 'We'd need a ladder. And then, if there's anybody else in the cell block they'd be liable to give the alarm. I guess we'll have to try the front.'

'I'm not very familiar with the layout of this place,' he added with dry humour.

Then went on: 'I don't want any shooting and I don't want any of us to be identified . . .'

'Nobody knows me in town, suh,' said Johnny Rayno. 'Let me go first.'

'All right,' grunted the old man. 'We'll be right behind you.'

They made their way to the front of the building. Both windows were shuttered but a faint chink of light escaped from one of them.

Johnny applied his eye to the crack. 'I can see one man at the desk. That's all I *can* see.'

'Let me have a look.' The old man took his place. Then he hissed, 'That's Joe Simms. He's just a deppity. I can't see anything else either. We can only hope Joe's alone. He'll need watching anyway – he's pretty quick on the trigger.'

'I'll watch him,' said Johnny Rayno.

'No shooting if you can possibly help it,' said the old man. 'We don't want the town around our ears. Pull your scarf up over your face, your hat down over your eyes. That gun-belt might give you away too. Take it off. Stick one gun in your waistband.'

Johnny did as he was told. Darkie Boots took the gunbelt. Ace-High was giving more low-voiced orders. Two men moved on ahead to watch the street. There was still a little activity sounding from the honky-tonks up ahead.

Johnny, suitably camouflaged, a gun in his right hand, reached the door of the sheriff's office. Ace-High waited by the window, his eye pressed to the crack. He was ready to give Johnny the signal if Joe Simms started to make any fast movements.

Johnny tried the door, it was not locked. Gently, one eye on the dark bulk of the old man, he lifted the latch. Ace-High gave no sign.

Johnny swung the door open, stepped inside. Joe Simms bounced to his feet, his hand dipping.

'Hold it,' snarled the masked man with the levelled gun. 'Get your hands up.'

Joe knew he wasn't fast enough to beat the speed of a lethal slug. He raised his hands.

Johnny Rayno had already ascertained, with an inaudible sigh of relief, that there was nobody else in the office. He made a circuit of Joe Simms and reached the door of the cell-block. There was no sound from back there.

He went behind Joe Simms, lifted his guns, told him to lie down on his belly. Joe cussed him, but a gun-barrel jammed into his spine made the deputy obey orders finally, and with alacrity.

In the desk-drawer Johnny found handcuffs. He cuffed Joe's hands behind his back, tied his legs with the man's belt, pulling his pants round his ankles too as an added precaution.

'If you try to yell you're a dead duck,' he said.

He blew out the lamp, crossed the room, opened the door. In the darkness which successfully blanketed their identities, Ace-High and Rafe Dawson filtered into the office. While they went on through to the cell-block Johnny took time to gag Joe Simms with the deputy's own kerchief.

There was no guard in the cell-block and the only other prisoner, a drunk by the smell of him, was snoring lustily. Sam Joubert was given a gun. He mounted the horse that had been brought for him. The whole bunch left the town quietly. It had all been so easy.

CHAPTER V

About a mile outside town the old man halted his troop. There were no sounds of pursuit.

Ace-High took out a bulky wallet and handed it over to Sam Joubert.

'That'll see you all right for a while, Sam. Get going. Don't come back.'

The ex-ramrod bridled as if he had been struck. For a few seconds he was silent. Then he burst out in hot speech.

'Don't come back! What d'yuh mean? I didn't kill that kid. Why should I . . .?' He paused again.

When he went on, his voice had risen almost to a screech. 'You believe I did kill him,' his head swivelled wildly, 'you all believe that! I shouldn't have come with yuh. I should've stood trial. You . . .'

Ace-High's voice cut in. 'Nobody's judging you, Sam. We set you loose tonight because we heard the nesters are out to lynch you. They're on their way right now. The time isn't right to buck everything, the law and everything right now. Your only chance is to run for it.

If you need anything write to me. Now get going!'

The old man's tone was implacable. Sam cursed and wheeled his horse. 'Maybe I will be back,' he yelled. He set his mount at a gallop and pretty soon the night swallowed him up.

'Phew!' said Ace-High. 'Whether he shot that kid in the back or not, he's certainly loco enough to've done.'

The bunch went on their way. They pulled on to the side of the trail as they heard other hoofbeats. Men drew their guns. 'Hold it,' said Ace-High quietly.

The riders, bound for town, swept past at a gallop.

Hoofbeats died away into the hot stillness. 'It was Jubel and his boys all right,' said Ace-High. He laughed, a gutteral sound. 'I wonder what they'll find when they get to town.'

'Mebbe they'll run into a posse before they even get there,' said Rafe Dawson as the Ace-High bunch started off again.

They reached the ranch without hearing any sounds of pursuit. Ace-High said, 'Johnny, when you've seen to your horse I want to see you at the ranch house. The rest of you hit the hay. You've been asleep all night, understand?'

The group broke up and a little while later Johnny went to where the old man awaited him in the study.

Ace-High said: 'I just wanted to enlarge a little on what I told the men. The law's liable to call here tomorrow. I want everybody to get their stories straight. None of us left the ranch. I want Cookie to back us up on that. My daughter will do the same if she is asked.

How Jubel Maxwell and his men have fared we don't know yet. Anyway, Jubel ain't going to be pleased about Sam Joubert's escape. Jubel's even liable to go off half-cocked and raid this place or some of the riders out on the range.

'I want you to see there's plenty of ammunition handy. No man must leave the ranch without his guns. Give any man who's riding alone an extra rifle and ammunition. I want a couple of scouts going the rounds of all the line-huts for the next few days, and bringing reports back to you. I want you to stay close to the ranch where they, and I, can get at yuh. We mustn't underestimate Jubel Maxwell. He's only got a small spread himself and his friends' places are even smaller, just stinking little holdings most of 'em, but all in all, Jubel can muster quite a force if he likes. A lot of 'em are Kansas men, and Kansas men ain't all sod-busters.'

The old man paused, though he didn't seem at all short of breath.

Then he went on: 'Don't forget Wyatt Earp does most of his free-wheeling in Kansas. So does Doc Holliday and Clay Allison. They've got another boy down there now, too, a younger one. He's made quite a name for himself. Maybe you've heard of him. Virg Craddock.'

'I've heard of him,' said Johnny, wondering what this was leading up to.

'Ever met him or seen him use a gun?'

'Nope. Just heard of him, is all.'

'I saw him once,' said the old man. 'Saw him kill two

men, beat 'em fair an' square. That was in Dodge City about ten years ago. I was running cattle down that way. Virg Craddock couldn't've been much above sixteen or seventeen then, a weedy little cuss, mean as Billy the Kid. A kind of boy wonder, cold as an old man with all his sins behind him, but with limbs that worked like greased machinery . . .'

Johnny was seeing a new side to Ace-High. He hadn't suspected the old man could be so gabby. And Ace-High was going on . . .

'Virg Craddock's rep has grown with the years. He travels around selling his gun. Nothing's too dirty for him to touch. Right now he's on his way here.'

Johnny was puzzled. 'You mean you've hired him?'

'No, but Jubel Maxwell has. Seems like they're old friends. That's something else I learned from Loopy. Virg Craddock will have heard of you, Johnny, so watch your step. I don't want any of the men to visit the town within the next few days. And, even when they do, I don't want any of 'em to go alone. That goes for you too.'

'All right, boss.'

The interview was over. Johnny said 'goodnight' and left.

He was walking away from the ranch house when a voice called his name softly. There was a flash of white by the kitchen door. He went over.

Amy said, 'You all right, Johnny?'

'Sure. Thanks.'

'I thought there might've been trouble.'

'No. No trouble at all.'

'Can I stroll with you a little way?'

'I don't think your father would like that. Particularly at this time o' night.'

Her white teeth flashed in the gloom. 'It's morning now. Dad thinks I'm in bed fast asleep.' A small warm hand was slipped into his and he let her lead him away from the ranch house.

They went over to the corral and leaned on the fence. He realized she still wore a dressing-gown, with only a short plaid blanket coat atop of it. Her legs were bare, her feet clad in the beaded mocassins she wore so much around the house. Her golden hair was coiled in braids around her small well-shaped head. In the gloom her eyes looked enormous.

As regards her apparel, Johnny knew she was quite warm enough: the air was still oppressive. But he could imagine what the boys would think could they see them together like this, Amy dressed the way she was. And the Old Man! . . . Johnny told himself he wasn't scared of old Ace-High. Or of losing this job (the first time he'd ever been a ramrod, at that) or anything. . . .

Still, despite the rough life he had lived, inherent in him was a sense of Texan chivalry towards the fair sex. He couldn't help wishing that – right now anyway – Amy was dressed a little differently.

But she made him forget all this when she came closer to him and gazed up into his face.

'What are you thinking about, Johnny?'

But he forced himself to say, almost mechanically, 'I'm thinking we might say Goodnight an' you ought to get back to bed. Or you're liable to be mighty tired in the morning.'

Her hands rested gently on his upper arms. 'All right, I'll go,' she said but she did not move. Her voice was a whisper; her face was lifted to him, a pale oval with enormous eyes and soft full lips like a dark bruise.

He grinned, a little tremulously and his arms went round her. He bent and kissed her.

They drew apart slowly, reluctant to do so.

It was then that they heard the shot. . . . Their bodies jerked and suddenly there was a gulf between them.

There was no other sound; no more shooting. Amy's eyes were wider than ever. Before she could speak, Johnny said quickly, 'Go back to the house. Go on. Run!'

'Yes.'

She left him.

There was no sign of life from the bunkhouse. Johnny drew both his guns, began to run, awkward and stumbling in his high-heeled riding boots.

He heard hoofbeats and for a moment he stopped running. The sound faded away quickly in the night and he was running again then; sweat burst from every pore of his body.

He almost fell over the body in the grass. A horse grazing nearby jerked its head and snorted at him. Then it went back calmly to its cropping of the grass.

The body was that of Sam Joubert. He had been shot cleanly between the eyes. His gun lay in the grass beside him. It had not been fired. Johnny had already pouched his own guns, and now he tucked Sam's Colt in between those two, in the waistband of his trousers.

He whistled softly to Sam's horse and the beast came willingly to him. He draped the body across the saddle. Then he led the horse back to the ranch.

Somebody heard him coming and a light went on in the bunkhouse. Then, as he got nearer, the bunkhouse door opened, releasing a gush of yellow brilliance. Rafe Dawson stood in the doorway, backing as Johnny advanced. Rafe's trousers were unbuttoned as if he had donned them in a hurry. His sparse red hair was tousled. He had a gun in his hand. He lowered this gently to his side. He wore no shoes and his feet were encased in red woollen socks.

Darkie Boots was out of bed too, barefooted, clad in long woollen underwear, the kind of stuff that most cowhands wore: it was warm in winter, soaked up the sweat in summer.

Darkie had a gun swinging at the end of a long arm. One or two more of the boys were on their feet. Others sat up in bed, blinking in the light.

'I thought I heard somep'n,' said Rafe Dawson harshly. He squinted suspiciously at Johnny. 'What you got your horse out again for? I thought you'd done enough riding for one night.'

'It ain't my horse. It's Sam Joubert's.'

'What's Sam come back for?'

'Yeah, I asked *myself* that.'

'It'd be simpler to ask Sam himself wouldn't it.' Rafe peered past Johnny, peered into the darkness and saw nothing. He began to look puzzled and suspicious again. 'Is Sam there? Is he?'

Johnny did not like Rafe's truculence. 'Yeah, he's there all right.'

'Well, what's the matter with him? Ask him to come in for Pete's sake.'

'He'll have to be carried in I'm afraid. He's dead.'

'Why, you . . .!' Rafe began to lift the gun.

'Don't be a fool!' snapped Johnny.

The ring of authority in the new ramrod's voice halted Rafe's movement. Johnny went on quickly, 'Come on, help me to get him in here.' He turned his back on Rafe and made for the door.

After a slight hesitation, Rafe followed him.

Between them, they carried the body in and, because every bunk was in use they laid it on the floor. The men, in different stages of undress gathered around it.

'By Gar,' breathed one. 'Clean between the eyes.'

Glances were thrown at Johnny. Rafe Dawson's look was now openly accusing.

Johnny drew both his guns slowly, held them out to Rafe. 'Check them! Smell them!'

Rafe hesitated, glowering around him. Then he took the two Colts, spun the chambers, smelled them, taking his time.

'Haven't been fired recently have they?' demanded Johnny.

'No, I guess not. But what's that other one in your belt?'

'That was Sam's. That hasn't been fired either.' Johnny handed it over. 'Seems like Sam didn't have a chance to fire it.'

Rafe inspected the third gun and gave the same verdict on it, if grudgingly, that he had given on the others. 'Sam said he'd be back. Everybody figured he'd be after you.'

'He came back. Mebbe he *was* after me. But somebody else got in the way.'

Johnny went on with the story. He left Amy out of it, of course, telling the boys he'd been coming back from his pow-wow with the Old Man when he heard the shot. The killer had got clean away. There was nothing anybody could do until daylight. Johnny said he wouldn't bother old Ace-High again tonight either.

Nobody argued with this decision, not even Rafe. Johnny got himself ready for bed.

Finally the light was doused again and, with their dead ex-comrade to keep them company now, the Ace-High boys slept.

CHAPTER VI

Sheriff Jamie Brown of Fishknife was a plump indolent character but a man not to be underestimated. He had been a lawman all his adult life and had made quite a rep for himself in the old days. Even now, in comparative old age (and when he could throw off his natural lethargy) he was liable to make decisions and stick by them. His old friend and deputy, Joe Simms was probably the only person Jamie, a confirmed bachelor, would trust as he trusted himself. Joe had the same kind of integrity.

That was why, no doubt, Jamie figured that he and Joe could guard Sam Joubert without any help from extra deputies. Yes, and handle any trouble that happened to come along too, him and Joe. But Jamie was away getting some supper when the Ace-High boys jumped the deputy. And when Jamie got back Joe had worked himself loose; though that was little help, as Joe didn't know who had jumped him and even his description of the masked man who held him up first was kind of garbled.

'So it could've been nester boys or Ace-High ones,' said Jamie. 'Whoever it was they certainly fooled us, pard. I didn't think any of 'em would make a set at the jail.'

'I guess they're clean away now whoever they were,' said Joe. 'I'm sorry, Jamie.'

' 'Twasn't your fault, boy. I shouldn't have been so goshdarned sure of myself.'

'I'm rarin' to go. They were quite gentle with me I'll give 'em that. If you want to hunt sign I'm right with yuh.'

'Take a swig of this coffee first. I'll . . .'

'Wait a minute.' Joe's hand was lifted. 'I thought I heard somep'n.'

'What! I didn't hear anything.'

'Sounded like somebody moving out back.'

'Mebbe it's Sam Joubert come back to give himself up,' said Jamie sardonically.

'I did hear somethin' I tell yuh.'

'All right then. What're we waitin' fer?' The sheriff hitched up his gun-belt, skirted the desk, opened the door which led to the cells.

The drunken prisoner was still snoring. 'Hell,' said Joe Simms. 'I forgot all about that cuss. I guess it was him I heard, huh?'

'Might as well make sure now anyway.'

'It kind of sounded like horses, at that.' Joe's gun was already in his hand as he followed his friend.

They passed the cell which housed the drunk, whose buzz-saw aria continued unabated. Jamie opened the back door. The men outside, who were in process of quietly dismounting from their horses were taken completely by surprise.

One of them got jittery and started shooting.

Jubel Maxwell and the sheriff cried out in unison. The one in rage, the other in warning.

Jamie dropped on one knee, drawing his gun. Joe Simms already had a Colt in his hand. But he did not have a chance to use it.

A bullet slammed into his chest and he died there in the narrow passage in the yellow lamplight where the drunk still snored as if peace reigned all around him.

One of the men out in the night screamed shrilly in agony ... Then Sheriff Jamie went down ...

Both the lawmen were still then. 'Leave them,' said Jubel harshly. 'Get the prisoner.'

But all the scrabbling men found was a drunken cowpuncher who snored in their faces and hardly twitched when they bawled their questions at him.

Now Jubel was almost incoherent with rage and frustration. Sounds of alarm were drifting in from the street and finally the nester leader had to yell, 'Let's get out of here before we have the town about our ears.'

The riders swept away, one man badly wounded, teetering in the saddle in the middle of the bunch.

Like the Ace-High boys before them, they got clear easily. About a mile away from Maxwell's holdings they split up and Jubel himself with two of his special henchmen went on together. The wounded man was a member of another contingent. The trigger-happy nester was a member of another bunch too, or Jubel might have plugged him out of hand. The fanatical smallholder was disgusted with the whole night's proceedings, knowing that the others probably blamed him for their failure.

What a bunch to work with! He was still seething when he bade his two pards a surly 'goodnight' (they slept in an outhouse) and went on to his cabin.

He was surprised to see a light in the window. Then the door was opened and his daughter stood there, a shapely form against the yellow light. Her name was Prue and she was nineteen. She should have been fast asleep long since.

Jubel threw his head back and bellowed, for he was a domestic tyrant. There were no words to the sound he made because his rage and frustration was boiling uncontrollably again. The girl vanished and Jubel threw himself from his horse and followed quickly.

He strode over the threshold of the cabin and the light half-blinded him for a moment.

Then he stopped dead.

Prue had retreated to a place beside the huge deal table. And beyond the table, lolling in Jubel's favourite armchair (the only one in the place) was a young man. His hat was on the back of his head, his legs were crossed nonchalantly; he rested comfortably on his spine.

His thumbs were hooked in his belt and he still wore his guns, both of them. His clothes were beaded and fringed in border fashion but shabby now, neutral-coloured. His face slanted up at Jubel, wedge-shaped, sallow beneath its tan, a scraped-bone look about it, predatory. There was no expression in the pale eyes beneath the light.

'Howdy, Jubel.' The man's voice was flat too. His lips hardly moved; he did not smile.

Jubel seemed to shake himself out of a trance. His rage had left him; he felt suddenly, curiously cold.

'Howdy, Virg,' he said.

'I'm afraid your daughter had to get up to let me in, Jubel,' said Virg Craddock.

Jubel looked at his daughter and saw her now, perhaps for the first time, as a young woman, a beautiful young woman.

'You can go back to bed now, Prue,' he said flatly.

'There's some coffee in the pot, father,' said the girl, and she went.

Jubel took a cup, poured one for Virg, noticing that the young man had already had one.

'I almost got lost,' said Virg.

He told of how he had met a jittery cowboy and shot him from his horse. Jubel wondered who the jittery cowboy had been.

He asked Virg questions but the killer couldn't tell any more – except that the cowboy was quite dead: Virg had dealt death too many times to mistake it.

A possibility of the identity of the dead man – 'a young man' Virg had said – entered Jubel's mind. But right now he kept this particular thought to himself. He'd know more tomorrow he figured: a death could not be hidden for long – unless somebody wanted to hide it. . . . Jubel glanced at the young man opposite him. Virg had no more compassion or conscience than a diamond-backed sidewinder, which suited Jubel's purpose admirably. But, also like a sidewinder, Virg had to be handled carefully, with gloves. Jubel said:

'We got a cot fixed up for you, Virg. I guess you won't mind bunking in the same room as my son, George.'

'Nope,' said Virg. 'But I'd like to hear about what you've been doin' tonight first.'

Jubel told him and, when the tale was finished, Virg said, 'It didn't go off so well did it?' He was a sharp one. 'Do you think the fellah I shot might've been the escaped prisoner? He kind of acted that way.'

Jubel had been thinking this and now he admitted it. But they decided to sleep on it anyway.

Deputy Joe Simms was dead. Sheriff Jamie Brown, a bullet in his side, would be laid up for some time. He lay cursing his fate, mourning the death of his friend, vowing vengeance and seething in helplessness and frustration.

Fishknife was without law.

Quickly, Lawyer Prom Varney nominated himself Mayor. It sounded more imposing than merely sheriff or marshal. Varney was the only person in town who knew anything about law, so the townsfolk went along with him. Approached on the subject, the crippled sheriff was quietly sardonic. According to him, Lawyer Varney was a jackass; so he couldn't do much harm anyway. If the townsfolk wanted a figurehead to give them a semblance of law, well, Varney was as good as anybody else. At least, he wasn't likely to go around shooting folks.

There was activity at the Ace-High ranch too. A toady from town, carrying the news of Joe Simms' death, wondered why he was not allowed past the gate. He could not know that the boys were giving Sam Joubert a Christian burial. And, because Sam should have been by now at the other end of the State, old Ace-High didn't want any outsiders to know about the change in plans, the internment.

This decision was strengthened when the old man heard of the Joe Simms killing. He didn't want his boys suspected of this. Jubel Maxwell was behind it, of course. Ace-High chuckled at the thought of Jubel's savage frustration at finding the cage open and the bird flown. But the old man was grieved to hear of the death of the deputy. Joe had been a likeable cuss. The nesters would have to pay for his death.

The old man decided he would lead a bunch of his men into town for the funeral of Joe Simms.

'And no trouble,' said Ace-High. 'If you see any of that nester scum, ignore them. Don't let 'em push you into anything. Let 'em gloat for a while if they want to. Our time'll come. I'm all through playing games. Once Joe Simms is decently buried an' kind of forgotten, it'll be war to the last man.'

The men listened, tight-lipped. They gave him their assurance to bide their time. But they knew what the latter part of the old vulture's pronouncement meant. Some of them had been in range-wars before. It was as if the internment of Joe Simms was to symbolise the end of law and order in Fishknife Territory.

And what would the new mayor, Mr Prom Varney, lawyer, do about this?

The town was full of people come in for the funeral. Most of the shops had their shutters up; dwelling-houses had their blinds drawn. Even the tough boys, sworn enemies of law and order in any shape or form, had forsaken the saloons and honky tonks. Even if they didn't mourn Joe's death, they had, at least, respected him in life. And now they paid him lip-service.

Fishknife mourned. Riding behind Ace-High and Amy as they led the ranch party along the main drag, Johnny Rayno couldn't help thinking of Sam Joubert and his unmarked grave on the edge of the valley. The townsfolk thought Sam had escaped. Many of them thought, no doubt, that it was Sam who had killed Joe Simms.

A funeral could easily lead to a necktie party: Fishknife was that kind of town. At the moment Sam Joubert seemed the most likely candidate for the loop. But Sam would never fill it. Why had he come back to the ranch that night? Who had killed him? These were questions that popped continually into Johnny's mind. And there wasn't a glimmer of an answer to either of them.

Over Boot Hill the skies were dark. There was no sun now but the air was oppressive.

All horses had been left below in the main street. The mourners followed the bearers with their burden up the stony slope to where Preacher Marks waited at the open grave and two men with a shovel apiece stood discreetly in the background.

There were flowers in profusion. A comely woman, flashily-dressed, but wearing a black hat was arranging the blooms. Her name was Minnie Prouty and she was the madam of one of the town's brothels. Tears were running slowly down her painted cheeks. She had been very fond of Joe. He had been one of the few 'real' friends she had in town.

The bearers lowered the white pine coffin. The mourners formed a circle which spread outwards and down the slopes. The preacher intoned the burial service.

Johnny Rayno didn't like the look of the preacher. Sour-faced old hypocrite, he thought. His eyes ranged along the ranks opposite him. Somebody nudged him and he turned his head to see Darkie Boots at his side.

'The lean white-faced cuss with the black clothes an' string tie – that's Jubel Maxwell.'

Johnny glanced at the Ace-High ranch's most bitter enemy. A mean-looking character all right!

But Jubel's companion interested him more.

'Who's the girl?' he asked out of the corner of his mouth.

'That's Jubel's daughter, Prue,' said Darkie Boots.

She was dark like her father but there the resemblance ended. Her face, framed in a cloud of jet-black hair, was heart-shaped and very beautiful. There was almost a Spanish look about it, as opposed to the Kansas angularity of her father. She could not be much above twenty, if that, Johnny figured. But her figure was superb. She was pretty tall for a woman, taller than Amy Logan. Johnny stole a glance at Amy, but she was looking at the droning preacher. When Johnny glanced across to the other side of the grave again it was to discover that the girl had moved. And he now found himself looking at the young man who had been standing behind her, who was now gazing at her with such intensity that he seemed oblivious of all else.

His face was pale and wedge-shaped, there was a wolfish look about him. He was evidently with Jubel and his daughter.

Johnny nudged Darkie Boots, indicated the young man. 'Who's that?'

'Never seed him before, Johnny,' said the mulatto tophand. 'But, boy, does he look a mean one.'

Mean was right. A sidewinder with twin guns. And in an instant Johnny realized who the young stranger must be. Virg Craddock, none other.

But the burial-service was over now and the coffin was being lowered into the grave and people were shuffling their feet, getting ready to leave. Jubel Maxwell turned and spoke to Virg Craddock, then twisted his head some more and spoke to another younker Johnny had not spotted before. And, just then, Darkie nudged Johnny again and said, 'That's Jubel's son, George.'

He was about eighteen. He was blockier than his

father or sister and he looked sullen, bovine, not at all dangerous. Just a kid with a chip on his shoulder.

'Come on,' said Darkie. 'You aiming to stay an' commune with the sperets or somep'n?'

Johnny turned, followed his friend. They joined the others at the horses below. The cavalcade set off back along the main drag.

The Ace-High boys studiously ignored the nesters. The nesters returned the compliment. Their respective leaders realized that to start trouble now, while the townsfolk were out in force and of uncertain temper, would be a mighty bad move.

Old Ace-High halted his men halfway up the main drag. 'I've got a couple of calls to make. Wait for me by the livery-stables an' keep out of trouble.'

He dismounted. His daughter started to follow him but he turned and said, 'You too, Amy.'

Johnny Rayno found Amy beside him and they sat in their saddles and watched the old man bull his way along the sidewalk and turn into one of the boarding houses.

'I guess he's going to see the sheriff,' said Amy. She was pouting a little.

They retreated to the corral, hitched their horses to the railings, dismounted. Some of the boys started tossing coins, betting on them. The old man didn't stay long with the sheriff. Johnny saw him come along the boardwalk again and turn into another doorway. A small shingle swinging out of the top of it was inscribed: *Prom Varney, Attorney-at-Law*.

So now Ace-High Logan was making a call on Fishknife's new mayor. Johnny's lips quirked mirthlessly. The old fox!

But the Old Man wasn't in there long either and when he strode into the corral he looked quite pleased with himself.

'Let's ride,' he said.

CHAPTER VII

Things went on pretty quietly at the ranch for the next few days. The boys were getting used to Johnny as ramrod. He knew ranch-work. He was a good man. He made decisions and he stuck to them.

The pugnacious red-headed Rafe Dawson was the best top-hand on the spread: Johnny had to admit this. So he made every use of Rafe and even this little hard-case began finally to show signs of genuine friendship.

The rains set in and as the temperature dropped tempers became more equable. There were no special instructions from the old man. The eagle had shut himself in his eyrie once more. Plotting again, no doubt. And, over on the other side of Old Slowcoach, was the nester leader, Jubel Maxwell, plotting too.

Johnny did not see much of Amy either. He had no occasion to go to the ranch house unless the boss sent for him and Amy didn't show her face outside more than once or twice. Maybe Ace-High was keeping her busy. Or was she deliberately avoiding him for some reason, he wondered? If so, this was contrary to her original manner. She had made the first move. She blew hot . . . and *now*, did she blow cold? He was a little piqued.

Then one night the Old Man sent for him.

Amy opened the kitchen door and greeted him affectionately. But she pushed him on through the passage, explaining that her father was impatient. When she let him into the study, Johnny was surprised to discover that Ace-High had another visitor.

He was a little man in black broadcloth. He had a toothbrush moustache and silver pince-nez which he put on the pinched little nose, scrutinising Johnny through them as they shook hands.

Lawyer Prom Varney, Mayor of Fishknife. He had a hand like a weak wet fish and, for a dry-as-dust legal man, he seemed rather ill-at-ease.

'Johnny – Mr Varney's got a proposition to put to you,' said the Old Man.

'Er – hum,' said Lawyer Varney. 'The legal position in Fishknife is er, Mr Rayno – is – er – irregular and far from satisfactory . . .' He got into his stride more. 'In my capacity of mayor I must supply law, but I cannot be a policeman too, you understand, Mr Rayno, I cannot be . . .'

'Tell him what you wanted to tell him,' put in old Ace-High gruffly.

Varney cast a rabbit-like glance at the bull-like hulk behind the desk. 'Um – yes. Fishknife needs a new sheriff, Mr Rayno. The admirable Jamie Brown will be laid up for some time. In fact, he may never be fit enough to take up his duties again. We want somebody worthy to take his place. I have been asked, in my capacity of mayor . . .'

'Hell,' put in Ace-High. 'What he's tryin' to tell you, is that he'd like you to be Fishknife's new sheriff.'

'Why?' said Johnny. And now he was looking at the lawyer again.

'Well, you have a – um – good reputation. You've been a lawman before.'

'I told him that, son,' said Ace-High. 'Deputy United States Marshal wasn't it?'

'Yes.' Johnny looked at the old man again. Prom Varney was staring into space; Ace-High lowered one eyelid in a ponderous wink.

'Can I have time to think it over?' said Johnny.

Varney came out of his reverie. 'Why certainly, Mr Rayno. Certainly.'

Ace-High rose, skirted his desk, put a heavy hand round Varney's shoulder and escorted him out. 'Johnny'll let you know as soon as possible. Don't worry, Prom.'

He was soon back. He said: 'Son, I've got the best interests of Fishknife at heart. To prove this I'm willing to continue paying you your foreman's wages even while you hold down the sheriff's job.'

'You seem pretty sure I'm gonna take the job.'

The old man's eyebrows rose in exaggerated surprise. 'Well, aren't you?'

Johnny smiled thinly, without mirth. 'All right, I'll take it.'

'You better go into town in the mawnin' an' get sworn in or somep'n,' said Ace-High laconically.

'You fixed it all right,' said Johnny flatly. It was a statement, not question.

But Ace-High chose to take it as a question. He looked peeved about it too. 'If you mean did I put in a good word for you, I did,' he said. 'I think you'll make a good sheriff. The kind Fishknife needs. New blood. Young blood. First-rate lawmen still don't grow on trees. They're rarer than good cattlemen. Rafe Dawson can handle your job here.'

'Rafe'll like that.'

Ace-High rose again. The interview was over. 'You can find your own way out can't you, son?'

'Sure.'

Johnny said 'goodnight'. As he went along the passage he reflected that things were certainly moving fast for him lately. Even faster than usual. First, ramrod of a big cattle-ranch, then a sheriff. All in less than a week.

He was so preoccupied that he almost ran into Amy before he saw her. She was standing in the gloom with her hand on the knob of the kitchen door. She opened it now, releasing a gush of yellow light, and passed through it.

'Want a cup of coffee, Johnny?' she said over her shoulder.

'Don't mind if I do.'

He sat down at the table. She did not turn but busied herself at the stove and he remembered the first time they had met in the kitchen like this. She was just naturally coquettish, he figured. And maybe that wasn't really such a bad thing in a woman.

He rose and went over to her, slid his arms around her waist.

She did not resist, only said: 'Careful, Johnny, in case father comes in.'

She gave a little gasp as he squeezed her. 'You'll make me spill the coffee. Go back to the table.'

Grinning, he did as he was told. She brought him a cup of coffee, and one for herself. She was flushed, her eyes shining, but whether from the warmth of the stove or some other reason he did not know. She looked very desirable.

He sipped his coffee, looked up. 'Seems I shall be leaving the ranch. Tomorrow probably.'

She looked startled. 'Why?'

'I'm going to take on the post of sheriff of Fishknife.'

'So that was the reason for Lawyer Varney's visit?'

'Yes.'

'It's a dangerous job.'

'I don't expect that carryin' a gun for the law will be any more dangerous than carrying a gun for Ace-High Logan.'

'No, I don't expect so.' Her voice was suddenly tart. 'That's your job isn't it: carrying a gun? I don't suppose who you carry it for is very important. Will the lawman's job pay more?'

'Could be,' said Johnny. He was still smiling but his eyes were cold and the girl felt herself go cold too.

'Maybe I shouldn't have said all that.'

He rose. 'No, maybe you shouldn't.'

He skirted the table, crossed to the door. She rose and followed him.

He turned suddenly and his arms went around her. He kissed her hard, brutally. Then he was gone into the night.

She closed the door, hit it with her clenched fist. 'The skunk,' she breathed. 'The skunk.'

Then she smiled at her own unladylike behaviour and went to ask her father if he wanted any coffee.

Johnny went into town in the morning and was duly sworn in. He elected to remain without a deputy until he could pick one he figured would suit him.

In Prom Varney's office he met a few more of the town's luminaries. He didn't take much notice of them right then. He figured he'd get plenty of chance to weigh them up, one by one later. They seemed a pretty uninteresting bunch anyway.

He got away from the stuffy atmosphere (he couldn't help feeling it was kind of hypocritical too) and made a bee-line for the lodging house where Jamie Brown lay. He was directed to the ex-sheriff's room. He knocked the door and a voice called 'Come in.'

Jamie sat up in bed. There was a gun on the bedside table within easy reach of his hand. Johnny liked the old man on sight. They didn't know each other, so he introduced himself.

They shook hands. 'I've heard of you, son,' said

Jamie. 'So you're the new sheriff.'

'Any objections?'

'Why should I have? I guess you can handle the job all right. You worked with Charlie Price in Tombstone didn't you?'

'Yes.'

'One of the best marshals in the West.'

'I know it.'

'But he died purty young.'

'A bullet in the back is no respector of age.'

'But you got the man who did it.'

'I did.'

'For that I thank you,' said Jamie Brown. 'I rode with Charlie Price in the old days when he was a kid. You remind me of him somehow, although then he was younger than you.'

'When I knew him some folks took him for my elder brother,' said Johnny.

'But he wasn't really old, just full of scars.'

'What are you tryin' to do: scare me out of this lawman's job?'

Jamie chuckled. 'I don't think you'd scare easy. Have a drink?' He reached a bottle from the side of the bed. 'There's a clean glass in the little cupboard.'

Johnny found the glass. Jamie fished his own glass from under the bed and poured out. They drank.

Jamie said, 'I heard a rumour you were just another of Ace-High's boys.'

'I was.'

They let it go at that. They had a couple more

drinks. They forgot Fishknife territory and talked about folks they had both known, they spoke fabulous names, many of whose owners were long since dead. Then finally Johnny got up to go and they shook hands again.

'Hurry up and get well, oldtimer.'

'I'll try, son. I'll try. So-long.'

'So-long.'

'If you ever want to know anything I'll be right here.'

'I'll remember that.' Johnny closed the door gently behind him.

He had the key of the sheriff's office but had not visited it yet. Not in daylight anyway. His lips quirked as he remembered the only time he had visited it. Then he became grave again as he remembered the sequel of that visit. The death of Joe Simms! A nester had been responsible for this: that was definite. But which nester? Johnny realized that in his new capacity of lawman of Fishknife he already had a couple of crimes to investigate. Two murders. Joe Simms; Sam Joubert. He realized the townsfolk would be quite happy about it if he blamed Sam Joubert, now ostensibly miles away, for the death of Joe and let it go at that.

But, as the finger of suspicion (at least, where some of the Ace-High boys were concerned) was pointed at Johnny himself, he figured he'd like to know who killed Simms. Though his investigations on that count would have to be very secret . . .

He realized he must find somewhere to live in town. He couldn't keep riding to and from the Ace-High ranch. Besides, that procedure, if followed, would be bound to cause unfavourable comment.

He halted outside Prom Varney's office. Then he climbed the stairs. The little lawyer was alone. Johnny asked him to recommend a good place to stay.

Varney sent him to the Widow Brent, a fat jolly woman who gave him a room and promised to look after him well. They agreed on terms.

She eyed his lean form up and down. 'It's time we had some real fast law in this town,' she said.

'I'll do my best, ma'am,' said Johnny. He left her, went on to the office.

The place was tidy, but it didn't have a used look. Evidently Jamie Brown had already had his own personal stuff taken away.

The cells were empty, the passage swept and clean. Here Joe Simms had died. Johnny unlocked the back door and went out. After the sun, the sky was dark again. A few large drops of rain fell. Johnny walked further, looking for signs, a clue. He found nothing. The rain began to come faster. He returned to the office.

He looked through the desk drawers. Wanted posters, a pack of greasy playing cards, a penknife with a broken blade. Then he made a circuit of the room, looking at other wanted posters, inspecting the locked rack of shotguns. The key to this was on the ring Varney had given him. He tried it in the padlock, turned it with difficulty. Jamie Brown was a good man, but getting old. Johnny told himself to remember to get a can of oil.

He sat in the rickety swivel chair, put his feet up on the desk. Widow Brent was expecting him back for lunch but there was time yet. He got out the makings and rolled himself a quirly, lit up. He sat in a brown study.

He smoked three cigarettes. Then he took out his guns and cleaned them. He decided he'd check the shotguns in the afternoon and oil all the locks and hinges in the place. He left the office, locking it behind him. He called at the hardware store right away, thinking maybe he'd forget on his way back, and bought a can of oil. Then he went on to sample Widow Brent's cooking, pronouncing it good.

The only other members of the household were the widow's old father, who acted as odd-job man, and two clerks from the local bank. One was a young sprig, an Easterner out here for his health, the other a meek, stoopshouldered middle-aged man called Anstruther. He'd been courting the widow for years. All she gave him was houseroom, he wasn't her kind of man.

Nobody said much. Everybody was weighing up the new sheriff. He was affable enough. He ate quickly and then went out to the pump to wash-up. He shouted 'So-long'. The door slammed behind him and he was gone.

'A young hellion,' was the widow's aged father's pronouncement.

CHAPTER VIII

Johnny carried on with his chores. He didn't go back to Widow Brent's for tea, but fetched some sandwiches in. Nobody came near him until night fell. Then things began to happen fast.

Footsteps thudded on the boardwalk. He had a gun in his hand when the door burst open. A scraggy cuss in jeans stood there, blinking. Johnny lowered the gun.

The character wheezed, 'There's a ruckus at the Silver Corral, sheriff. You better come down there. . . .'

Johnny rose, reached for his hat. 'Lead the way, friend.'

The Silver Corral was Fishknife's largest saloon, a long building with a garish false front, illuminated now by wavering yellow naphtha flares. Johnny covered the distance in long strides, the blue-jeaned character hopping and skipping at his heels.

A few other folks converged on the saloon from various directions. As Johnny got nearer he heard the hubbub from inside. He hadn't heard any shooting yet. He kicked open the batswings, strode through. Then he stopped, legs spread apart, hands poised over the butts of his guns.

Folks were packed in a circle. Heads turned. 'It's the new sheriff,' said somebody. The ranks broke and Johnny saw the cause of the trouble.

The girl was leaning against the bar. Her face was white, her eyes enormous beneath the cloud of dark hair. Jubel Maxwell's daughter. What was her name? ... Prue! She was hidden from Johnny's sight for a moment as the two men, locked in mortal combat, staggered past her. One was her brother, George, the other an Ace-High cowhand called Maxie, an oafish individual that Johnny Rayno hadn't had much to do with.

Young George, now no longer bovine, was giving a good account of himself. A table went over. The two men broke apart. Maxie grabbed a bottle from the bar, threw it and missed his mark. The bottle almost hit the girl, flashed on, smashed a mirror behind the bar. In retaliation, young George threw a chair. It caught Maxie a glancing blow and sent him spinning.

Maxie fell flat. He jack-knifed slowly to a sitting position and went for his gun. George, the sod-buster's son, pulled another trick out of the hat. And, with a speed that made folks gasp, his gun was levelled before Maxie's had even cleared leather.

'Drop it, kid,' snarled a new voice.

Maxie's life hung in the balance. Then slowly the muzzle of the gun dipped.

'Drop it, I said!'

George dropped it.

'That goes for you too, Maxie. Don't try any tricks or I'll blow you apart.'

Maxie took out his gun, tossed it to the boards. And George turned now to face Johnny Rayno, who stood with a gun in each hand.

'What's it all about?' asked Johnny. Softly now.

'He insulted my sister,' said George Maxwell. He was breathing hard, but showed no other signs of strain. He wasn't mussed about much either. Johnny realized he had made a mistake in his earlier estimation of the youth as just a surly slowcoach. That draw of his had been really something.

'The boy's telling the truth, Sheriff,' said a voice behind Johnny. 'Maxie was drunk. He called the girl a little nester bitch. A man worth his salt don't make war on women. The boy took him up on that.'

Johnny looked at Maxie, now on his feet. Maxie scowled, said nothing.

'I guess it's safe for you to pick up your gun now and pouch it,' said Johnny.

Maxie bent, picked up the gun, slipped it into his holster. Johnny looked at the younger man, who returned his glance sullenly, but now it seemed, without rancour. 'You too.'

And George retrieved his own gun.

'Get out of here, Maxie. Get out of town!'

Maxie shuffled his feet. 'You cain't do this to me, Johnny.'

'I'm doing it. Unless you'd like to stay an' make a play.'

'Not me.' Maxie had seen Johnny in action. He shuffled on; nobody tried to stop him and he passed through the batswings. A few seconds later his horse's hoofbeats clattered off into the distance.

Johnny looked at George, at the girl.

'Thank you, Sheriff,' she said.

He said: 'I don't think your brother needed any help, miss.'

George smiled. It was the first time Johnny had seen him smile: it had a grudging quality, as if the face was unused to smiling. 'She's thanking you because you stopped me from killing the skunk.'

'So I did.' Johnny holstered his guns. 'Let's take it easy from now on, huh?'

He turned and strode from the saloon.

He was at his desk when another knock came on the door. This time, however, the knocker did not enter right away and Johnny called 'Come in'.

George Maxwell came in. Johnny looked for his gun. But George strode on, hands well away from his sides and said, 'Jest want a friendly pow-wow, Sheriff.'

'Sure. Take a seat.'

George twisted a small chair around, straddled it. 'You want a deppity sheriff?' he asked, direct.

'Why, you nominating yourself?'

'Somep'n like that.'

'You're kinda young.'

'I'm over eighteen. Plenty old enough. You've seen me work. Ain't I fast enough?'

'You're fast enough.'

'I'm not dumb either.'

Yeah, boy, I certainly had you figured all wrong, Johnny told himself. Aloud, he said:

'I don't think your dad would like it.'

'To hell with my dad. I'm fed up of him telling me what to do, what to think. I'm fed up of being treated like a kid.'

Johnny let that ride for a while. 'Where did you learn to draw an' shoot?'

'I taught myself. Out in the hills. Other places. Odd times. Any place where it was quiet an' lonely. I told myself a man needed that if he wanted to stand shoulder-to-shoulder with other men. I told myself I'd never use my gun unless I was pushed – I've seen too much o' that.'

'Shoulder-to-shoulder with some men. But better than most, huh?'

George's sombre face lit for a moment. 'Maybe.' Then darkened again. 'Maybe I wanted to be better than my dad.'

'Why? You aim to shoot him someday?'

George smiled again. 'No. He could be plenty worse, I guess. But he don't give me credit for a mind o' my own. But I've got a mind – an' it don't think the same way his does....'

George raised his hands, groped at the air inarticulately for a moment. Then he went on, strongly:

'That thing back in the saloon a while ago, that was a personal thing. If you hadn't happened along I probably should've killed that skunk. And wouldn't have regretted it either. But I can't get het-up over possessions and land the way my dad does. I couldn't hate a man because he has more land than me, the way my dad hates Ace-High Logan. Hate has poisoned my dad's life for years, made my mother's life a misery. But she hates too now: anything or anybody he tells her to hate. I want to get out o' there before I grow the same way. . . .'

The door was knocked and he paused; the door opened and his sister came in.

'I'm ready, George.' She looked past him at Johnny then.

'I want to thank you again for what you did, Sheriff.'

There was warmth in her voice, warmth and beauty in the whole presence of her. No hate here either, he thought, and was curiously enlivened. He said:

'I did nothing, Miss Maxwell except what I had to do.'

'That's it. Sometimes a man just has to do just that,' said George. Half-turned towards his sister, he looked back. 'What do you say, Sheriff?'

'Twenty-four hours. Then, if you still feel the same, come back an' we'll see the mayor.'

'Thanks. I'll be back.'

They said their 'goodnights'. Johnny was left alone again.

The first incident happened that very night. But Sheriff Rayno did not hear about it until the following morning, after a man-sized sleep at Widow Brent's in one of the softest beds he'd occupied for a long time.

He was at the office when the two middle-aged nesters burst in. He didn't know either of them and they were too incensed to introduce themselves properly. But their tales were plain enough.

They were neighbours, occupying smallholdings side by side near Old Slowcoach about three miles west of Jubel Maxwell's place. Last night their fences had been smashed, their gardens trampled, their outhouses, barns and hay stacks burned to the ground by a bunch of masked horsemen. The only place that hadn't been touched were their living-quarters where they slept with their families.

'They were Ace-High men,' one of the nesters almost screeched.

'Did you see any of them?'

'Not properly. They were there an' gone in no time. But they must've . . .'

His companion, a little more sober now, broke in: 'They came in two bunches. About half-a-dozen in each I guess. One bunch attacked my place.' He jerked a thumb. 'The other attacked Jeb's place at the same time. They lit torches – threw them. They were there an' gone before we could hardly get our pants. We took shots at them but I don't figure we hit anything.'

'Recognize any of 'em?'

The man laughed sardonically. 'Not a hope.'

'Ace-High men! ' put in Jeb, parrotlike.

Johnny Rayno looked at him. 'Did *you* recognize any of 'em?'

'Wa – all – no. But . . .'

'Lose any stock?'

'All of it. Cattle.'

Both men had lost all their stock they said, what there was of it. Johnny's first feeling, although he concealed it, had been one of utter savagery. How had Ace-High dared? And on the first day of his (Johnny's) duties as sheriff, too . . . !

But now Johnny became puzzled. What would AceHigh want with poor nester stock? Stuff so easy to trace too, against Ace-High full-blooded stock! And why would Ace-High attack small cattlemen too, when his fight was mainly with the sheepmen?

'How much was there?' he asked.

Not much they said. They were poor men. The ground was bad there too, they said. They had water, but little else. Their neighbours' sheep had made short work of the grass.

'We couldn't find any tracks,' said one of the men. 'The ground's hard. Sheep had made it harder.'

Now Johnny spoke his thoughts aloud. 'Why would Ace-High Logan want to run off your cattle?'

'To ruin us,' burst out Jeb. 'Even if he ran 'em till they were dead.'

'Maybe Ace-High's men did it without him knowing,' said the other man, whose name it seemed was Harry. He seemed to have a sneaking regard for old Ace-High.

The reason for this was explained in his next words: 'I was a big cattleman myself once till I fell ill and lost everything. I came to this neck of the woods to start afresh. I may be only a nester but I hate sheep just as much as Ace-High does. I don't think Ace-High's the sort to run cattle to death.'

Johnny didn't think Ace-High was that sort too. But what really did he know about Ace-High? The old man was fanatical, ruthless. He hadn't built a cattle empire with kid gloves. Wouldn't he do almost anything to achieve his own ends?

Johnny buckled on his gun-belt. 'First thing I'd better do is go out an' inspect the damage.' He led the way from the office.

Curious glances followed them as they rode down the main drag. But nobody spoke. Once on the trail, they set their horses at a gallop.

The raiders had indeed made a mess of the two little spreads. They were a porridge of charred timbers and black ashes, with the living quarters rising starkly out of the desolation. Ace-High Logan, though ruthless, was not the sort to make war on women and children, Johnny reflected bleakly. Were those blockhouses, still standing among the blackness, sardonic evidence of Ace-High's guilt?

Johnny, who had learned his tracking at an early age, began to look for signs.

He had no luck whatsoever until he was some distance away from the two small spreads. Looking back, he could see the two ranch houses – if ranch houses they could be called – like toy boxes in the distance. From here, they were so close together they looked like one ranch; and a pretty small one, at that.

Johnny could see tiny black figures moving about back there and he knew they were Jeb and Harry and their families vainly trying to salvage something from the chaos. Johnny Rayno, hard-boiled troubleshooter, was strangely moved. But he reflected that it was a good job this hadn't been Injun work or there would have been nothing standing and those figures would be lying stark and scalped. No, this was white man's work all right. Though that was little consolation to those people or, indeed, to him.

He turned his head again. Sunlight glinted on something in the brown grass. He halted his horse and dismounted. He bent and picked up the metal object.

It was a large silver coin with a hole in the centre. A Mex (or Spanish) *peso*. The hole had been punched in artificially but very painstakingly and neatly. No thread adhered to it but Johnny figured it had probably been attached to somebody's clothing. A man's fancy vest or chaps or sombrero. Or even used as a watch-fob; or to ornament a kerchief; Johnny had even seen South American *vaqueros* with coins on their boots or as part of the pinwheel spurs they affected. This ornamentation was more likely to belong to a Mexican or an Indian; although Johnny had seen white American waddies and such like wearing them.

He dropped the drilled *peso* into his vest-pocket and, half-bending, hunted for more sign. He found nothing else right then. He had, however, been able to follow the meagre tracks left by the tiny herd of cattle as they were driven off. These signs were so small in the stunted brown sward that they had gone unnoticed by the two nesters, not so well-educated in the ways of the trail as Rayno, ex-Injun fighter. Now he remounted his horse and followed the trail until it petered out altogether.

Up ahead, shimmering in the damp haze, so that they looked like a mirage, were a small range of hills. Perhaps the cattle had been driven through there, Johnny reflected, and on into the rangeland immensities beyond, where they could be sold easily to many of a dozen small spreads, brands blotted expertly, no questions asked. If the stock had brands at all, Johnny promised himself he'd ask the two nesters about this.

He would also, he decided, take a look in those hills as soon as possible.

But now he turned his horse and set off back the way he had come and pretty soon was back at the two smallholdings and the people vainly trying to salvage something from blackened chaos.

Johnny called the two men to one side. He showed them the drilled *peso* and asked if either of them knew or had seen a Mexican, an Apache maybe, or anybody else wearing such an ornament.

They said they hadn't.

But then Harry said suddenly, 'Wait a minute though. How about that greaser who works at the livery stable. He wears some gosh-awful clothes. Seems to me I've seen him in somep'n with shiny things on it.'

'You mean the one they call Pedro?' said Jeb.

'Yeah, that one.'

'Yeah. He's like a clown,' said Jeb. 'An' a dirty clown at that. But he's little more than an imbecile I guess.'

'He don't have to be no professor to ride with a wild bunch,' said Harry, without cracking a smile.

Johnny said:, 'I'll take a looksee at this Pedro character anyway.' He dropped the drilled *peso* back into his pocket, patted the pocket. 'Don't mention this to anybody.'

'We won't,' said Harry.

Johnny remounted his horse. Harry stood looking up at him, went on talking. Johnny had taken a liking to Harry, who was far less hysterical than his neighbour. Harry's brand of plain talking was the kind that Johnny liked to hear. Consequently, he was not at all antagonised by Harry's next words; he was glad Jeb hadn't spoken them in his waspishly insulting manner or he might've had to slap the runt down.

But there was Harry, looking up at him fearlessly – spouting: 'Sheriff, we heard you were an Ace-High man.'

'I was,' said Johnny. 'But I was a law-officer too, before I ever met old Ace-High.'

'We heard that too,' Harry admitted.

'Any questions?' said Johnny.

Harry shook his head slowly. His gaze was direct. 'We hope you'll help us all you can, sheriff.'

'I will.' Johnny turned his horse's head, flipped a hand in farewell.

'We'll hold you to that,' Jeb called truculently after him.

Johnny did not look back. He set his horse at a gallop and did not ease off until he was passing the corral of the Ace-High ranch.

CHAPTER IX

Rafe Dawson came out to meet him. Johnny wondered why Rafe wasn't out on the range. 'The boss in?' Johnny asked.

'Yeah. I guess so.'

'I want to see him. Maybe you better come along too.'

The old suspicious look came back into Rafe's eyes. But he said 'All right' and tagged along.

Johnny led the way to the front of the ranch house, climbed on to the silent verandah, rapped on the frame door.

He was relieved when it was opened by Ace-High himself. He didn't want to see Amy if he could help it. Not right now, anyway.

The old man smiled, carolled, 'Johnny Rayno. Hallo, Johnny. Is this a social call or an official one?'

'An official one, suh.' Johnny jerked a thumb. 'That's why I asked Rafe to come along too, in his capacity of ranch foreman.'

'Oh,' said Ace-High. But he still smiled, his hawk-like eyes watchful but carrying a twinkle. He stepped aside. 'C'mon in, both of yuh.'

They followed him into his study. The house was silent. There was no sign of anybody else being there. Johnny couldn't help wondering where Amy was. Had Ace-High been expecting him he wondered.

The old man sat down in his swivel-chair behind the desk. The two other men sat on hard chairs on the other side of the desk, opposite him. 'Shoot, Johnny,' said the old man.

'Coupla nester smallholdings were burned last night. Outhouses, feed, everything like that. The raiders let the living quarters alone. Considerate, huh? Nobody human was burned. Stock was run off.'

'Sheep?' asked the old man.

'Cattle. Poor stock by all accounts.'

'Yuh think we did it...!' burst out Rafe Dawson.

The old man held up his hand. 'Wait a minute . . . Go on, Johnny.'

The sheriff took the drilled *peso* out of his pocket and placed it on the desk. 'I found this.'

Ace-High picked it up, inspected it. 'None of my men wear this kind of ornament. It's probably Mex or Injun. We ain't got a Mex or Injun. There's Darkie Boots but I don't figure he wears anything like this.'

'It could be a lucky piece to be carried around,' said Johnny, who had only just thought of this possibility. The field was widening alarmingly.

Ace-High said: 'You ever seen one of our men with a piece like this?' He gave the *peso* to Rafe Dawson.

The pugnacious little foreman turned the coin over

and over in his fingers. His brow dark, he glanced at Johnny. 'No,' he said.

'Set on any new men recently?'

'No,' Rafe handed the *peso* back, his movements almost violent.

'Anybody do any riding last night?'

'Only the usual night-riders. Everybody else was in the bunkhouse. I can vouch for 'em.'

Rafe didn't seem as if he was lying, Johnny reflected and Ace-High hadn't had time to brief him. Though, of course, they could have been expecting a visit from the law. Then there would have been plenty of time to get their stories straight. Everybody at the ranch could have been thoroughly briefed by now.

'How do you know the night-riders didn't leave their posts and go wide-looping?'

'We don't,' said Ace-High sharply. 'How many do these nesters figure were in the bunch of raiders?'

'Uh, about a dozen.'

'We didn't have that many night-riders out,' said Rafe Dawson. 'An' they were split up all over the place.'

Ace-High brought his hand down on his desk-top with a faint smack. 'I hate the sheepmen. Why would I want to attack cattlemen?'

'They own slices of land. On top o' the creek too.'

Rafe Dawson half-rose. 'Boss . . .'

'Hold it.'

The little man subsided, muttering. He couldn't figure why the Old Man was being so kid-glove with this upstart, even though Johnny had been the Ace-

High foreman; for a very short time at that.

But Ace-High was looking at Johnny very levelly, totally unsmiling now.

'If I swear that I had nothing to do with that raid will you believe me?'

'Yes, I'll believe you!'

'I swear!'

So that was that. A few seconds later Ace-High let the two men out. He shook hands with Johnny. 'If you need any help,' he said. And he left his sentence unfinished.

Johnny, as he rode away, felt kind of frustrated. He set his horse at a gallop. On the way back to town, he didn't see a soul. It was a somnolent moon when he rode down the main drag of Fishknife. The clouds were overcast and there was threat of more rain. Not that it wasn't needed. The heat was oppressive. Men lounged on the sidewalks, tilted in chairs. Bonneted women went about their business.

Johnny turned his horse into the narrow cutting which led to the livery stables, a place he had only visited once before and that was when he first hit Fishknife. Now he kept his horse in the little stable at Widow Brent's place. When the hostler ran forward to grasp the horse's bridle, Johnny waved him away.

'Where's Pedro?'

The man looked puzzled but said, 'He's out back, Sheriff, I'll call him for you.'

'That's all right. Just lead me to him.' Johnny dismounted from his horse, looped the reins over a hitching-post. He followed the hostler through the gloom of the stables and out into the yard at the back.

Pedro was grooming a horse, humming a Spanish lament. He was a little dark man in dirty shapeless jeans. He wore no hat and his long black hair fell in lank strands as he worked. A more *un*-ornamental specimen would have been hard to find: Johnny began to think he had drawn a hell of a wrong card this time. He called the man's name.

Pedro's reflexes were dull. He was slow to turn, his movements unco-ordinated, ungainly. His eyes focused badly too and first of all he seemed to be looking at a point way off somewhere at the right of Johnny. And, even when his eyes reached Johnny there was a kind of blank look about them.

'Howdy, Pedro,' said Johnny. 'I'm the new sheriff.'

Light flickered in Pedro's eyes, went off again. 'I seed you, Sheriff,' he said in a curiously reedy voice.

Johnny wasn't quite sure what he meant – probably he already knew about the new sheriff, probably he had already seen the new sheriff walking along the street or something.

'I want to talk to you, Pedro,' he said and went nearer.

Pedro's jeans were pulled together by a length of frayed rope tied in an enormous knot. He did not seem to be wearing a weapon of any kind.

'Right,' said Pedro. 'We talk, Sheriff.'

Johnny strode towards the dilapidated fence at the back of the yard. He motioned Pedro to follow him and the little Mex did so. Johnny hunkered down against the fence and Pedro followed suit, placing himself at the side of the sheriff but a few feet away from him. Even so, they looked quite companionable squatting there.

Johnny looked at Pedro some more. He remembered what Jeb, the nester had said about Pedro being like a clown. A clown in gaudy finery? Pedro's dark wizened blank-eyed face with its wide mouth, its lank, tangled black hair might be a little clownish. But the rest of him was strictly rags and bones.

Johnny was beginning to wish he hadn't been so curt with Pedro's boss, that he had asked that worthy some tactful questions before he came on through to the back. He couldn't quite figure this little dark ageless-looking man who sat staring at him so intently and yet not seeming to see anything. Subtlety had never been Johnny's strong point; he figured he'd try and find out just how dumb this character really was.

'They tell me you like fancy clothes, Pedro,' he said.

'*Sí*. Clothes. You got some fancy clothes, sheriff?'

'Not particularly.' Johnny stabbed a finger at Pedro's outfit. 'An' I wouldn't call that fancy either.'

Pedro's face opened in a grin that threatened to split his head in half. What few teeth he had were brown and crooked. He stank of unnamed foods, the spicy stuffs his sort loved. 'Thees,' he said. 'Ees for work. For work. *Sabe?*'

Now he thinks I'm the one who's dumb, Johnny reflected. 'Yeh, I *sabe*,' he said. 'You only wear your fancy clothes at night, huh?'

Pedro nodded his head vigorously, grinned some more. 'Sure, sure. At night!'

'Did you wear fancy clothes last night?'

'Oh, sure.'

'Where were you last night, Pedro? Where did you go?'

'Was weeth Santos. All night was weeth Santos.'

The law didn't scare Pedro it seemed. He was smart enough to spout an alibi when one was needed. Or had he just answered a simple question, being too dumb to know its implications? Who the hell was Santos anyway? Johnny wondered.

'I'd like to see your fancy clothes sometime, Pedro,' he said. 'Maybe we could do a trade or somep'n.'

'You buy me a drink I show 'em to you,' said Pedro, like a monkey begging for nuts.

Johnny thought fast. He produced a bill, held it out. 'I haven't got time to come with you. You go spend this on drink, huh?'

'The boss . . . ?'

'I'll fix it with the boss.'

'*Gracias, señore* sheriff,' Pedro was already on his feet. With a last bob and a grin, he scuttled away.

Johnny rose. He heard Pedro's boss yell after him and he went on through. 'Let him go,' he said. 'I want to talk to you.'

Pedro hadn't heeded his master's voice anyway, and was out of sight. 'All right,' grunted the man, looking puzzled. 'Come on in here, Sheriff.'

He led Johnny into the harness room which smelt not unpleasantly of oil, leather and horses. Johnny forestalled any questions by quickly asking one of his own. 'Where does Pedro live?'

'Live?' The man loked even more puzzled. 'Waal – he lives here I guess. He sleeps in the little cubby in the back.'

'Does he keep his fancy clothes in there too?'

The man smiled uncertainly. 'Why – yeah.'

'I'd like to take a look. Make it fast. That's why I wanted Pedro out of the way.'

Once more the man led the way. 'Pedro not in any trouble is he?'

'Not yet,' said Johnny cryptically.

The 'cubby' was a box-like room with one tiny dirt-encrusted window. It had a bunk against the wall and a single rickety chair. In a corner was a tall old wardrobe. Johnny opened the door.

Pedro had quite a collection of finery for a man of his means. Unless he had another source of income apart from his menial job in the stable. That was a thought!

Still waters ran deep!

Pedro was still all right, unruffled. Was that only because, as seemed the general opinion, he had no mind to speak of, or was he a consummate actor with a colossal nerve?

Johnny's theories were galloping away with him. He was disappointed to find that Pedro's taste in ornamentation, despite the fact that the man was a greaser himself, ran more to Indian-style than Mexican. All beads and frills and fancy stitchwork. No pesos or anything remotely resembling them.

'How long has Pedro been in this territory?' asked Johnny.

'He was here when I came,' said the hostler. 'An' that was over twenty years ago. Fishknife was just a trail-stop then, hadn't even got a name. Pedro was just a kid. So was I, if it comes to that. I'm only a bit older than him. He was working in these same stables. They wuz owned then by a man called Batey Jones. After my paw died, Batey married my maw. Then both my maw an' Batey died – an' that's how the stables came to belong to me. Is there anything else you'd like to know, Sheriff?'

'Just about Pedro that's all. Did he have any folks?'

'If he did I never seed 'em or heard about 'em.'

'Was he always dumb the way he seems to be now?'

'In the early days I guess he didn't seem any dumber than most kids his age. Just kinda slow. Being a Mex, nobody took much notice of him. He just don't seem to've grown up properly.' The hostler shook his head slowly from side to side. 'He's good with horses. He talks to them more than he talks to humans. But even I can't figure him sometimes and I've probably known him as long as any man in this town.'

'Who's Santos?' Johnny shot out the question.

The hostler seemed suddenly disconcerted. He licked his lips. Then, after a moment he said, 'Santos keeps the *cantina* on the edge of town.'

'An' Pedro goes there?'

'I dunno. I suppose he does sometimes. Santos is a Mex. He's quite a power in Mex circles.'

'In what way?'

'They seem to look up to him. Maybe he's better educated than most of 'em. I guess he's well-heeled too.'

The hostler dried up. Either he didn't know much about this Santos or he didn't intend to say much. Johnny bade him *adios* and left the place.

He called at Widow Brent's to leave his horse at the stables there. Then he went on to the *cantina*, entered its cool dusky interior.

There were not many people in there and Johnny saw Pedro right away. He could hardly miss him : the wizened stableman was draped over the bar directly opposite the door; a shaft of sunshine illumined his squinting face as he turned it slightly and saw Johnny.

He put down the glass he was holding and threw his hands in the air. He almost lost his balance but the bar held him up.

'Ah, thees ees my friend, the Sheriff!' he cried. '*Señor* Santos, I want you should meet my good friend, the Sheriff.'

He twisted his head again and now Johnny saw more fully the man behind the bar. He was fat and swarthy and there were tiny gold rings in his ears.

As Johnny got nearer he realized how really big the man was. That wasn't all fat by any means – there was a lot of muscle there too. The man's shirt – pale blue silk, though a little dirty – was open almost to his waist and a gargauntan chest was revealed, a mat of black hair.

Santos had black sideburns down almost as low as his jawbones; his hair was curly and pomaded and, although he was probably ten years older than Johnny, there wasn't a hint of grey in its glossy blackness. His face was fleshy but had a hawk-like cast too; he wore a well-trimmed moustache which just fell short of being a handlebar. He grinned and his teeth were large and white. Despite his bulk he was a handsome devil and Johnny figured he probably got on well with the ladies.

'I am glad to meet you, Sheriff,' he said and held out a huge hand.

Johnny took it. There were iron sinews beneath that soft pad.

'Glad to meet you, too,' he said.

'What will you drink, Sheriff? It is on the house.'

His voice was well-modulated, forceful. It had an accent, but none of that pidgin English quality that characterised the speech of Pedro and many others.

Johnny said, '*Tequila*, please.'

Santos beamed again. 'You like *tequila*?'

'If it's good *tequila*.'

'The Santos *tequila* is the best in Texas,' boasted the fat man.

He was right too.

Johnny quaffed it and looked about him. There was nothing suspicious about Santos either, though he could be a dangerous man if he chose, Johnny figured. And Pedro, he was half-seas-over, and looked less like the conventional plotter or villain than the Man in the Moon.

Poor Pedro! He turned to Johnny now and burbled, 'You want see my fancy clothes now, huh?'

Johnny didn't say he'd already done so. Out of the corner of his eye he was watching Santos. Santos was not grinning now but the monumental flabbiness of his face was as handsome and inscrutable as an Indian chief's.

Johnny said, 'I've got to go see a man, Pedro. I'll come and see your clothes tonight shall I? You'll be at the stables won't you?'

'*Sí*, I weel be at the stables.'

Johnny left the cantina. He wondered why he had come there in the first place. He hadn't asked Santos whether Pedro had been at the cantina last night. He couldn't very well have done so, not with Pedro standing right there. Even if he had taken Santos on one side he thought he knew what the answer would have been, whether the truth or not. That was a Mex place and Mexicans stuck together.

CHAPTER X

There was little more to do that day. Eat, have a yarn with the boys at Widow Brent's, get acquainted more with the ins and outs of his new office. Then at teatime the storm broke. Like a huge stampede it was, black, thundering, the sound of it almost terrifying. The raindrops were as big as marbles but they quickly mingled, making a solid sheet. In a trice the main drag of Fishknife was empty of any living thing. Not even a mangy cat or pariah dog.

Within minutes the street was a river of black slimy shifting mud.

By nightfall the fury of the storm had spent itself, but the rain still fell steadily. Men and beasts, coming into town or leaving it for home, floundered in the treacly mud. A wagon with two horses got bogged down completely. It took six men to get the equipage free. Slicker-clad employees of the saloons and honky tonks were laying duckboards across the mud, improvised pathways, leading to the doorways of the establishments. Men braved the rain now, treading gingerly on the duckboards, making for the bright lights, the clank of piano. the clink of chips, the gurgling of liquor, the playful squeals of percentage girls.

Johnny Rayno was buckling on his gun-belt, preparing to go out, when there was a knock on the office door.

The door opened and George Maxwell came in. Johnny remembered then; remembered George had wanted to be deputy. George had kept his promise to come back. And he answered Johnny's unspoken question now.

'Yeah, I still want to be deputy.' He smiled thinly. 'I had a riproaring row with my old man. I'm bigger'n him. Finally he said to hell with me.' George spread his arms wide (he was quite an eloquent young man once he got going). . . . 'So here I am!'

'All right,' said Johnny, adding darkly, 'An' mebbe I'm gonna need you. C'mon.'

He led the way. A few minutes later they were ensconced in the sitting-room at the back of the office of Prom Varney, Lawyer, Mayor of Fishknife. They reclined in armchairs with glasses of whiskey and the little lawyer, also in an armchair, was trying very hard not to give a direct answer to the sheriff's question.

Things were gettting complicated, too complicated even for his tortuous legal mind. As always, for beneath his pomposity, he was a small-minded soul, he was on the side of the Big Noise. The Big Noise in Fishknife Territory was still Ace-High Logan and Varney liked to keep on the right side of that old warhorse. He still looked upon Johnny Rayno as an Ace-High man.

But surely the big youth, this George Maxwell, was one of the other side? And the sheriff wanted him (Varney) to swear the youth in as a deputy, and was pretty insistent about it too.

The whiskey, and it was good stuff too, didn't seem to be having a mellowing effect on the sheriff at all. He was still looking at Varney with those cold eyes of his, eyes that Varney could imagine staring at him over the barrel of a gun, eyes that sent cold shivers down the little lawyer's spine.

Varney hadn't actually objected to swearing in George Maxwell as a deputy. He had just side-tracked the thing a few times, had been as ambiguous as he possibly could, so ambiguous in fact, that he had gotten tangled up in his own rhetoric and, finally, dried up. And then when the sheriff suddenly rose to his feet, the little lawyer almost jumped out of his skin.

Johnny said flatly, 'All right, let's get on with it. We've got work to do.'

So – George Maxwell, ex-nester, gunfighter, got himself sworn in as deputy sheriff of Fishknife.

At least, reflected Prom Varney wryly, after the two men had left him, the law was now a very representative one. So representative of both factions in the Fishknife feud, in fact, that it could cause alarming complications. Prom decided finally that old Ace-High ought to know about this new move on the part of his puppet lawman. Maybe the new lawman wasn't a puppet after all – he certainly didn't act like one. The little lawyer took a couple more drinks to fortify himself then he went out and got his horse.

If Ace-High Logan was at all peeved about his pet lawman's sudden idiosyncrasies he didn't reveal the fact by word or gesture. 'Don't worry about it, Prom,' he said.

He very graciously gave the lawyer a mite of supper before seeing him on his way. Even so, as he wended his way back the way he had come, Prom was a frustrated man. He had been patted non-commitally on the back like a good but foolish dog and told to go on home. Prom's small spirit spouted a flicker of rebellion. Well, he had done his best to keep the peace. So, now to hell with 'em – to hell with 'em all!

He was wet, too. It was still raining. Not heavily now, but a depressing drizzle. The night was very dark. No stars; the moon hidden behind black clouds. His ride was a lonely and depressing one.

Until – suddenly – the riders came.

He was deep in his depressing thoughts; the wind blustered; he was not aware of them until they were almost on top of him.

He screamed with the suddenness of it all and reached for the derringer he carried in the waistband of his pants. A swinging fist buffeted the side of his head, knocking him sprawling from his saddle. He rolled in the wet grass, dazed, terribly frightened.

Rough hands hauled him to his feet. It was too dark for him to see who his attackers were. This was like something out of a nightmare, dark shapes all around, closing in on him. Men and horses were intangible, huge; terrifying creatures of the night.

Had not hands held him upright, Varney would have fallen again. One of the attackers had found the derringer.

'A popgun,' said a voice and there was a gruff spurt of laughter.

Varney did not recognize the voice. He was by now too bewildered and scared to recognize anything. He wondered what was going to happen to him.

A match was scratched, the flame held so close to his face that he started backwards. 'Hold still!' A fist jabbed into his back, jolted him forward, brought scalding pain. He had a glimpse of two eyes squinting at him maliciously, a slice of unidentifiable face.

'It's the new mayor,' said a jeering voice.

Then the light went out; and the night was blacker and more terrifying than ever after it.

'He's one of Ace-High Logan's lapdogs,' said another voice. 'He's just coming back from there. I saw a nice tree back along apiece. C'mon, let's not waste time.'

Another voice said, 'You can't do that, Virg, that'll mess things up. If we . . .'

There was the sound of a blow. The first voice spoke up again, laden with a cold hating fury that froze the wretched captive's blood.

'Name no names. I've told yuh – name no names!'

The name hadn't registered on Varney's mind. The name of a dangerous man, answered now in quavering tones by the transgressor, who had taken the blow and bowed before it. 'I – I'm sorry. I didn't think.'

'In future, stop to think,' said the cold voice (its owner seemed nearer to Varney now), 'you'll live longer that way.'

Varney was still wondering what they would do to him, whether the cold-voiced man would have his way. He could already feel the rope around his neck; the breath choked in his throat . . . He sensed rather than saw the sudden movement of the man in front of him; he tried to jerk backwards but the hands held him and something smashed into the side of his head. The night was suddenly lit by a gush of red . . . then there was nothing else.

Johnny Rayno was awakened early the following morning by Widow Brent. The sheriff was wanted – was wanted urgently.

George Maxwell had gotten himself a room in the widow's establishment. Johnny raked him out too. Buckling on their gun-belts, the two lawmen hurried out into the street, down to the office, where already a small bunch of men were gathered.

Darkie Boots detached himself from the group and hurried forward to meet Johnny, fell into step beside him, telling his story as he did so.

Rounding up Ace-High strays early that morning. Darkie had come across a saddled riderless horse then, about a half-mile further on, the prostrate body of a man.

It was Lawyer Varney. He had been beaten up terribly and, at first, Darkie thought he was dead. However, he was at Doc Jupp's place now and still alive, though unconscious.

Johnny spun on his heel. 'We better go down there.'

'Wait a minute,' said the coloured ranny. 'There're some more people here to see you.' He jerked a thumb. 'Nesters. A coupla their places wuz attacked last night. I'm glad you came when you did – I didn't like the way them ginks wuz eyeing me. They seem to think the Ace-High did the job.'

Johnny had halted. 'And did they?' he asked flatly.

'No.'

'But you were out night-ridin'.'

'No, just early this morning. I was at the ranch last night. Nobody went out 'cept the usual quota of night men.'

'Those smallholdings,' said George Maxwell, silent until now. 'Was my dad's . . . ?'

Darkie turned on him. 'I don't think so, no.'

Next moment they were in the midst of a voluble bunch of nesters.

Johnny raised his hands, bawled, 'Quiet, all of you. Let's take it slow.'

The babble died. Johnny went on quickly. 'I want to see the ones directly concerned in the office. Rest of yuh stay outside.' He turned. 'Darkie. You go down to the Doc's an' wait for me there.'

'Right, Johnny.' The coloured ranny turned on his heels.

'That black coot's an Ace-High man,' bawled one of the nesters. 'He was out on the range. He . . .'

'Stow it!' snarled Johnny. 'Name-calling won't get you anywhere.'

Darkie had turned, hand poised over the butt of his gun. He had stood enough.

'All right, pardner,' said Johnny gently. 'All right.'

'All right, Johnny,' echoed Darkie and relaxed a little. His eyes found the face of the loudmouthed nester, seemed to be memorising every lineament of it.

'Keep out of my way, punk,' said Darkie tonelessly. Then he turned and started to walk again. The loudmouthed nester did not move. He had gone a little white around the gills.

Two men followed Johnny and George into the office. Johnny was reminded of the visit of Jeb and Charlie, here for a like purpose such a short time ago. And these two had the same look: their hard, careworn features working with a bottled-up rage. And, once inside the office, they exploded into furious speech.

Their story emerged. The old story. Fire, wreckage, destruction, pillage. Riders swooping down in the night, working quickly, ferociously. Then soon gone.

But this time a man had been killed!

A man?

A lad! Sixteen years old.

Awake in the night with toothache. Hearing the marauders far sooner than anybody else did.

Grabbing a shotgun and running out into the night.

To be shot down like a dog.

'My son,' said the elder man of the two, brokenly. 'But he got one of the skunks. I'm sure he got one of 'em.'

'How sure?'

'Pete – my son – he was alive when I got to him. He said he had seen one of 'em fall from his horse. He looked like a Mexican – had a big hat. His friends picked him up, took him with them . . . Pete wasn't able to tell me any more . . .'

George Maxwell was pouring drinks. Now he handed them round. 'Sit down,' he said, gently, to the two older men. 'Take it easy for a bit.'

Although the men were obviously puzzled at seeing George as a deputy, he was one of their own sort and they obeyed him. Maybe it wasn't true, after all, that the sheriff, this lean, hard-eyed young man was an Ace-High puppet. George Maxwell, son of the most fanatical Ace-High hater of them all, seemed to trust this man, look up to him.

The sheriff said: 'Can either of you remember anything else that may help?'

They took their drinks, shook their heads, bemusedly.

'Did you lose any stock?'

This goaded them into speech again. They had lost stock all right. All of it.

The old man whose son had been killed: he raised horses. They had all been run off.

The other man had a few sheep, and also pigs, horses, cows, poultry. A farmyard conglomeration.

Johnny Rayno, a cattleman born and bred, could not kill a spurt of disgust at such a mixed (and smelly) menage. His horses and cows had been run off, his pigs and sheep shot, his poultry burned in its cots.

Neither of these men were out-and-out sheepmen. The older one, in fact, hadn't had any sheep at all, wasn't too keen on them he said.

Johnny was puzzled.

He made his decision, said: 'First thing we'll do is go down to Doc Jupp's an' see if Lawyer Varney's fit to talk. Maybe he ran into these raiders an' it was them who beat him up. We might have something to go on then, huh?'

The other three men assented; Johnny led them out, through the sullen crowd outside.

At the little frame house on the edge of town they were greeted by Doc Jupp and his buxom wife, who had been a nurse during the Civil War. Prom Varney, Darkie Boots sitting quietly beside his bed, was still unconscious.

The little lawyer was badly battered. The doc and his wife were doing their best but neither of them would be surprised if Varney never came out of his coma.

The law was frustrated again.

'Let's ride,' said Johnny. 'We'll call in on our way back, doc.'

Some time later, with the two nesters in attendance they were surveying a depressing and now all-too-familiar scene.

The rain drizzled miserably from darkened skies, hissed on black smoking timber, black earth, small butchered animal bodies.

And in one of the cabins (the two men were very close neighbours) a mother and her friend mourned over the murdered body of her son.

Johnny Rayno had seen much of this kind of thing. He had seen Injun work of a far more terrible kind. But with these people he felt like an alien. His cynicism had left him. He would have to do something about this. He left George with these people (they trusted George) and rode away, looking for sign.

But the rain had done its work well. He found nothing, not even a drilled *peso* this time. Evidently the wounded raider – Mex or not – had been gotten away all right.

He returned to the smallholdings, collected George. They left the nesters to their wreckage and their grief. They rode on to the Ace-High ranch.

CHAPTER XI

First of all they went to the bunk house. Darkie Boots had got there before them and was having a meal before going out on the range. The only other person there was George's old enemy, Maxie, who was laid up with a busted wrist. They glowered at each other. Johnny wondered how Maxie had got his wrist. Maxie was the sort of blustering coward who would pick the night to cloak his nefarious deeds.

Cookie clattered pans in the kitchen. The rest of the boys, ramrod Rafe Dawson included, were out at their various tasks.

Johnny didn't think Maxie would try any funny stuff. The big oaf had already seen how fast George could move. He left George talking amiably with Darkie and went on to the ranch house.

The frame door was opened by Amy, who looked surprised to see him, a sudden flush staining her smooth cheeks.

'Johnny!'

'Hallo, honey.' The endearment slipped too easily

from his lips. 'Is your dad at home?'

'Yes, he's in his study. Working on overdue accounts or something he said.'

'I want to see him pretty importantly.'

'Oh, that's all right. He'll see you. What's the matter, Johnny?'

'Nothing you need worry your purty head about.' He backed her into the kitchen. She stamped her moccasined foot.

'Don't talk to me as if I were a child, Johnny Rayno. There's something the matter. This is an official visit. I can see it in your eyes.'

'What else can you see in my eyes, *chiquita*?' he said and bent and kissed the tip of her nose.

She smiled and smacked him lightly on the cheek. Then her face become grave again. 'Tell me, Johnny.'

He made his decision; said, 'A couple more small-holdings were burned out last night. A man was killed. A boy, really, only sixteen. A plucky kid who tried to take on the whole bunch of night-riders on his lonesome.'

She made a sharp intake of breath, drew back from him a little. 'You don't think . . .'

He went on quickly: 'Did you hear a bunch of the boys ride out last night?'

'You do . . .' She did not finish. Her face was suddenly frozen. She went on coldly, 'If they did they were pretty quiet. You don't have to ask me whether dad went out or not. He didn't. If he gets up in the night I always know about it. I'm a light sleeper and, strange though it might seem, I worry about him sometimes.'

'I worry about him sometimes too,' said Johnny tonelessly.

She looked at him as if she didn't know what he meant by that. He wasn't quite sure himself what he meant by it.

'I'll go through to your dad shall I?' he said.

'If you like,' she said. 'You know the way.'

She was too far away now for him to be able to touch her. She seemed withdrawn. He turned and opened the door and went out into the passage and made his way to the Old Man's study. He rapped on the door and the Old Man called 'Come in' and he opened the door and entered.

Ace-High looked up from his desk, a litter of papers and ledgers and envelopes. There was nothing strange in his manner, no hint of surprise in the expression on his hawk-like face. No expression really: inscrutable as that of an Indian chief.

'Howdy, Johnny. Glad you came. I was just making up the wages. Sit down.'

Johnny sat down. Ace-High pushed a bulky envelope across the desk to him. 'Here's yours.'

Johnny fingered its bulges and they crackled sweetly. But he did not pick it up.

'I'm sorry, suh,' he said. 'I can't take it. Not while I'm sheriff. The way things are, it ain't right.'

Ace-High's face was suddenly old. 'Maybe you're right.' He leaned forward across the desk. 'But you came to this territory to work for me an' you wouldn't have taken on the lawman's job if I hadn't kinda pushed yuh. I still look upon you as on the payroll. I figure you'll get tired o' this lawman's job sooner or later an' when that time comes, I want first call on yuh. I want you back here as my foreman again.'

He stopped. Johnny said nothing. He didn't know what to say. Their eyes met, locked inarticulately. Then they both looked at the desk, at the package lying there. Ace-High reached out and took it, dropped it into a drawer.

'What's on your mind, Johnny?' he said.

'Two more smallholdings were raided last night,' Johnny blurted out. 'A man was killed.'

Ace-High sat back in his swivel armchair. His face was grave now as well as old.

'Is that why you wouldn't take the money, Johnny?'

'I don't think so. When I first took this job I guess I was kinda cynical about it. I guess I figured the Fishknife law was slated to be just another offshoot of the Ace-High empire. I was quite prepared to take all I could get. Since then I've changed my mind. Maybe that's because I've met some of these nesters an' got to like 'em.'

The old man smiled wryly. 'Maybe I ain't so cynical as I used to be either,' he said. 'Maybe I'd get to like some of them nesters too, if I had a chance to meet 'em . . .'

He paused. Then he looked straight at Johnny. 'What do you want me to do now – give you my assurance that I did not send – or lead – any of my men out shooting up nesters last night?'

Johnny smiled now. Talking to this old buzzard was like playing poker with a sharper with two pair of hands. 'If you like,' he said.

He went on to mention the beating-up of Prom Varney. Ace-High said that Darkie Boots had already reported this.

'Prom had been to see me,' said the Old Man. 'He had a tale to tell about you. Evidently he's got you taped as an Ace-High man same as everybody else. I guess, right now, I don't like that cut-an'-dried kind of thinking no more than you do. Prom thought I ought to know that you had taken on a nester as your deputy.'

'A nester no longer,' said Johnny. 'If ever I saw a man cut out to be a real conscientious lawman it's young George Maxwell.'

'More power to the boy,' said Ace-High. . . . 'I wish I knew who'd jumped Prom Varney. He's a mealy-mouthed little cuss but he never did anybody any real harm. It certainly wasn't any o' my boys.' Once more he leaned forward over the desk. He went on:

'When I sent for you in the first place I had some scheme at the back of my mind about trying to drive the nesters out altogether, those damn sheepherders anyway – I'll admit that. But since then, particularly since you took on this sheriff's job an' started to get so conscientious about it, I began to think well what's the use. Let 'em live. As long as they don't foul *all* my land up, let 'em stay. I ain't as young as I used to be, Johnny.

Nesters I could fight maybe, but I ain't aiming to take you on as well, son.'

Johnny made another of his lightning decisions. He unpinned his star, hefted it in his hand. 'You don't have to take me on too,' he said. 'I'll quit this lawman's job.'

And suddenly Ace-High wasn't so old.

He thumped the desk.

'Oh no, you won't,' he bellowed. 'You'll pin that star right back on your chest an' continue to be proud of it. There's a job to be finished. Somep'n mighty nasty is goin' on in Fishknife territory. You can have all the help you want from me, even if it is to get some stinkin' sheepmen out of a hole. D'yuh want some men right now?'

'Maybe Darkie Boots that's all.'

'He's a good man – and your friend. You can have him.'

The old camaradie was back between them. And some time later they got up and shook hands and then Johnny left.

Amy was waiting in the kitchen, her face taut and white, her eyes enormous.

'It's all right, *chiquita*,' he said softly. 'Everything's all right.'

When she spoke her face was against his chest and her arms gripped him.

'I'm so glad. You didn't understand did you, Johnny? You didn't understand. Dad's never treated any of his men the way he treats you. He's never talked about anybody the way he talks about you. He's a man's man,

Johnny. I know that, no matter how much he dotes on me, he had always wanted a son, too. You're not much older than me, are you, Johnny. Don't you realize that if Dad had had a son he might've been like you.'

When the two lawmen got back to town they discovered that Prom Varney, though alive, was still unconscious. They had a meal at Widow Brent's, then they split up.

Many people still did not know that George Maxwell was a deputy sheriff. He took off his badge and slipped it into his vest pocket. It would soon be dusk; the eating-houses and honky tonks were beginning to fill. He browsed around. These townsfolk, most of whom did not know of his sudden elevation to officialdom, looked upon him as just a nester kid. They took little notice of him and, even if they did, were not suspicious of him as they might've been of the new sheriff.

George heard a drunken Mexican telling about a man that was laid up bad in the Santos *cantina*. That could mean plenty, or nothing. George did not push his luck. He went back to the office to report to the sheriff. Johnny had not returned. George sat and smoked and waited.

Boot-heels clattered frenziedly on the boardwalk. George was on his feet, gun in hand, when the door crashed open. It was a man George knew vaguely by sight: the hostler from the livery stables. He was unarmed, his hands flapping when he saw the gun, his mouth opening and shutting, fishlike.

George holstered the gun. 'What's eatin' you?' he asked coldly.

The man found his voice. 'The sheriff! I want to see the sheriff.'

'He's right here.' And there was Johnny now, in the doorway behind.

He came in, closed the door. The hostler whirled on him. 'It's Pedro. I found him dead . . .'

Johnny's mind worked fast. 'Shot?'

'No, knifed.'

The listening George wondered whether the Mexican laid up at the Santos *cantina* had been shot. But he didn't even have time to make his report as he followed Johnny and the sweating hostler down the street.

There was a little knot of people outside the double doors of the livery stables. They parted to let the law through. In the lamplit interior Doc Jupp was on one knee beside a bundle in the straw.

'I hadn't seen him since purty early last night,' babbled the hostler. 'I didn't worry then. I figured he'd got some money from someplace and gone off on a drunk or dressed-up in his flash duds to hunt himself an Injun gal down by the crick. I expected to see him this mawnin' but he didn't turn up – his crib hadn't been slept in. Even then I didn't worry – it wouldn't be the first time Pedro had dolled himself up an' gone on a two-day bat. Then, just now, I was forkin' over some feed – an' I found him . . .'

The hostler's voice was suddenly choked with sobs.

He had had a bad shock. He had gotten attached to his strange little sidekick over the years. Tears ran down his leathery cheeks.

'. . . They had buried him deep beneath the straw.'

'I reckon he's been here since sometime last night too,' said Doc Jupp.

The bottom layer of straw was saturated with blood. Pedro's finery was red-splashed, gaudy. Pedro's head had been almost severed from his body. He lolled, a dried-out husk, grinning up at them. Gently, the medico covered him with a horse-blanket, a filthy shroud.

Doc Jupp rose. 'There was nothing in his pockets, Sheriff, nothing at all.'

Johnny Rayno said nothing. He was staring at the brown bundle. He was remembering that last night he had promised to come and see Pedro and he hadn't been able to make it. Would he have found Pedro alive and would Pedro have been able to tell him anything? Would he, in some way, have been able to prevent this? Had Pedro been killed to keep his mouth shut or was there some other reason?

The local undertaker and his assistant arrived and the wizened body was taken away. The bloodstained straw was forked over and sifted. Nothing was found. The straw was taken out in the yard and burned. Doc Jupp went home. The gawping sightseers drifted away in twos and threes: there was nothing more to see. The hostler was sat down, given a drink and told to take it easy. Johnny and George began to go over the stables.

They finished up in Pedro's two-by-four cubby. Neither of them had found anything. They sorted among Pedro's meagre belongings and his fancy but trashy clothes. Pedro had travelled flashily (when he had travelled at all) but he had travelled light. He had left nothing of his life behind except his shoddy and pitiful finery. No clue as to who had killed him or why.

The ground all around the stables was trampled and muddy. If there had ever been any signs outside that might have told some kind of tale they had long since been obliterated. A monotonous drizzle of rain still fell. It was hardly noticeable now, people were so used to it. Everything – the weather, the recent black nights, Pedro's own reputation for strangeness and unreliability had been in the murderer's favour.

This day, reflected Johnny Rayno, had begun with reports of violence. It was certainly ending the same way.

And it had not ended yet for as the sheriff and his deputy left the stables, preparatory to widening their investigations, a man accosted them.

He was breathless, had evidently ridden hard. As they moved out of the gloom of the alley, Johnny Rayno recognized the elderly smallholder called Harry whose little spread had been the first to be attacked.

'Sheriff, Jubel Maxwell and a big bunch o' the boys are ridin' on the Ace-High ranch . . .'

Harry stopped; he was gawping at George Maxwell. The sheriff didn't seem to notice this, he snapped:

'It's mighty funny you should be the one to come an' tell me this.'

'What's he doin' here?' Harry jerked a thumb at George.

'He's my deputy. An' particularly unbiased, believe me.'

'That's right,' put in George. 'Let's hear your story. Whether my father's mixed in it or not, I'm still on the side of the law. Every time!'

His vehemence seemed to convince Harry. He had got his breath back by now too.

'Like I told you before, Sheriff, I used to be a rancher in quite a big way myself till I fell ill an' lost everything. I hate sheep as much as Ace-High Logan does and I can't help admitting I have a sneaking regard for that old mossyhorn. I hoped he wasn't behind the raid on my place, although I couldn't figure who else could be, I had to find out one way or another. And I don't mind admitting, right now to your face, Sheriff, that if I proved to myself that old Ace-High was behind the raid on mine and Jeb's place, I meant to kill the old skunk, whatever the consequences might be. So I started to sleep by day an' go out at night an' watch the Ace-High ranch. I was there last night in them trees on the knoll overlooking the place. I was there all night, wide awake. I didn't see any bunch of horsemen leave. Then when I heard this morning that there'd been a coupla more raids I knew Ace-High couldn't've been behind them.'

'That makes sense,' said George Maxwell.

Harry went on: 'The word came around this morning that Jubel Maxwell was holdin' a meetin' at his place. Me an' Jeb went along. It was a fighting, lynching, big-talking meeting. A lot of talkin' was done by that Kansas gunman, Virg Craddock. The man gives me the creeps . . .'

George Maxwell spat. 'Is he still staying there? Dad said he'd got to find a billet someplace else.'

'I don't think he's actually stayin' there,' said Harry. 'Cain't say where he is staying now. But he's allus there when there's trouble brewing. I guess a range-war 'ud suit him and his sort. Plenty of shootin' an' killin' an' lootin'. . . .'

'So what happened?' said the sheriff.

'I told 'em what I thought but they wouldn't listen to me. They're gonna meet at Jubel's place at midnight an' ride on the Ace-High spread.'

'So I better be at Jubel's myself at midnight,' said Johnny succintly.

'That goes for me too,' said George.

Johnny looked at him and said nothing. Harry said 'I'll come with yuh. So will my neighbour, Jeb. He's down in the Silver Corral waitin' right now.'

'You surprise me,' said Johnny drily.

'Aw, Jeb's not so bad. He hated Ace-High as much as any of 'em. But he's a logical man an' my friend an' he believes what I tell him.'

'We'll get ready to ride,' said Johnny.

They met later at the sheriff's office. Harry was accompanied now by little Jeb, sullen as ever, but quite tractable. Then the door was rapped and there was a surprise visitor, Darkie Boots, also raring to go.

After Johnny had left Ace-High back at the ranch he had returned to the bunkhouse to discover Darkie had polished off his meal and already ridden out on his duties.

Darkie had only recently got back, he said, and the Old Man had sent him in to join the law. He hadn't needed any orders: it would give him almighty pleasure to ride with Johnny and his friends.

They mounted; rode out of town.

CHAPTER XII

The little one-eyed hunchback, Loopy Kenwood, watched the horses. The men had filed into the house. The small living-room was packed to capacity. Mrs Maxwell and Prue had been ordered to stay in the bedroom. They obeyed orders because there was little else they could do. Both of them had tried to dissuade Jubel from his bloodthirsty conclusions. But in vain.

Now they sat in the darkness and listened to the bloodlusting voices in the other room and Mrs Maxwell said:

'Maybe we could've done somep'n if that Virg Craddock hadn't been talking pizen into your dad's ears all the time. There's something evil about that young man.'

'Yes,' said Prue. 'I'm glad he left here and went and lived someplace else. The way he used to look at me made my flesh creep.'

'I wonder where he's living now,' said Mrs Maxwell.

Loopy Kenwood who, that morning, had been

purposely sent on an errand to town to get him out of the way, hadn't known about the impending raid until right now. It was too late to go and warn his good friend, Ace-High Logan.

Or was it?

If he jumped on one of these horses right now and rode. Rode hard...

But he knew that as soon as they heard the hoofbeats the whole pack would be after him. His misshapen body was awkward in a saddle. A horse, perhaps because it sensed his deformity, his awkward seat, would seldom respond to his urgings. Even the most inept man in that cabin now was a far better horesman than Loopy Kenwood. No, even if he picked the fleetest horse....

But, if he led a horse away gently, and did not mount until he was out of earshot of the cabin...?

... Though they were making a lot of noise in there, as if preparing to leave. Probably they would come out before he got out of earshot. Then he would be shot down like a dog. He shuddered when he remembered Virg Craddock's cold eyes upon him. That one might be already suspicious. That one would kill on the slightest provocation, enjoying that, always enjoying it....

But if, Loopy reflected (and Loopy was far from as crazy as people thought him to be)... if he let the horses go now, if he stampeded them...?

He could tell those folks in there that something had scared the beasts, a prowling wild cat maybe, who had run away too. He could roll in the dust and yell, pretend the horses had bowled him over, he could even knock his head on a stone until it bled.

He was so taken up by this idea that he began to peer around him in the darkness for a likely stone.

He didn't think Virg Craddock could kill him for this. He didn't think that the other men, enraged though they would be, would allow Virg to do this. Maybe they would beat him . . . but Loopy was used to kicks and blows. He could stand that. And they would have to round all the horses up before they could ride and perhaps, during the ensuing melee, he would be able to slip away and ride to warn his good friend, that grand hard-bitten old gentleman, Ace-High Logan. . . .

Loopy was so immersed in working out this plan, the best he had thought of yet, getting ready to put it into operation, that he did not hear the man approach from the darkness until the man was almost on him. Then he was warned and he turned, but it was too late: a strong hand was clapped over his mouth, the hard muzzle of a gun ground into his ribs.

A voice hissed in his ear, 'Take it easy, old timer. This is Johnny Rayno. I'm Ace-High Logan's friend too, remember?'

The man might've been reading his thoughts: a great surge of relief flooded through Loopy. He saw now others moving out of the darkness. Here was salvation! He nodded his head vigorously and Johnny let him go.

'You've come to stop them?'

'Yes, I warned the law.' Loopy saw that the voice

belonged to a nester called Harry, a man he liked. Harry's pardner, Jeb, was there too : sullen but reliable. And Darkie Boots! And George Maxwell ... If only George's father, Jubel was like this boy and his sister ... 'Have you a spare gun?' said Loopy.

'Yes, I think so,' said the sheriff.

'Give it to me, please, I want to help.'

'Give it to him,' said George Maxwell, and the sheriff handed over a spare Colt.

He began to give out with orders in a quiet incisive voice.

'George an' me an' Darkie will go in through the front. Harry an' Jeb you come in through the back. As soon as we're in, oldtimer ...' this to Loopy, 'you bust the living-room window an' cover 'em from there.'

There were murmurs of assent.

'All right,' said Johnny. 'Let's go.'

The hostler, whose name was Grimes, missed his sidekick, Pedro more than he would have thought possible. Pedro had never talked much, but except for his periodical sorties on the town, he had always been there, somewhere in or around the stables. He had hummed softly or whistled as he groomed the horses. Old Spanish tunes that he must have heard some time, probably way back when he had been a child.

Grimes was not a fighting man, nor a particularly brave one. But he figured that, as Pedro's best friend (probably the only *real* one he'd had in Fishnife) he should follow Western tradition and get the man who had murdered his pardner.

Grimes had his suspicions. Pedro had been very thick with Santos of late. The big flashy owner of the *cantina* had seemed to exert a powerful influence over the little horse-handler. An evil influence Grimes had thought. Grimes didn't like Santos. It was well-known that Santos was a rich man. Grimes was sure Santos hadn't got all his money just from running a cantina. Fishknife was not very far from the borders of Mexico. Lots of things went on along the border and on its other side.

Had Pedro found out too much about Santos' nefarious activities and been killed to keep his mouth shut? Santos was ruthless and cruel, he would think nothing of slitting a man's throat.

Grimes, whose stables were a kind of sounding-board for local gossip, had heard that there was a sick man laid up in an upper room of the cantina. A wounded man maybe? Was there any connection between this sick man and the murder of Pedro?

The sheriff had been talking to Pedro too. Had been asking questions about him. Had been very nosey.

Well, the sheriff would be kept out this time. . . . Grimes crouched in the wet darkness out the back of the Santos cantina and watched and waited. He wore a dark green waterproof slicker. Under the slicker, in his right hand, he held a cocked gun. If he discovered that Santos or one of his men had murdered Pedro, he meant to avenge Pedro's death. How he would be able to discover the killer he did not know. He had already tried the back door of the *cantina* and found it locked. All the windows were securely fastened too. So, Grimes just watched and waited and hoped....

The sounds of revelry came through to him from the front of the place.

But, as he stood there cramped and wet in the darkness, gradually the sounds died and he knew, though he had forgotten to bring his watch, that it was very late.

Then, finally, his patience was rewarded.

Light suddenly blossomed in a back window of the *cantina*. It was just a faint shaft and Grimes realized that the window was heavily curtained: even this seemed to add to his suspicions that there was dirty work afoot. He had had an idea that something would happen tonight. He forgot the wetness and discomfort. He flexed his limbs, tightened his hold on the gun hidden beneath his slicker, made sure that the folds of the slicker were draped correctly and there was a convenient gap to allow him to aim the gun quickly and, if need be, start shooting.

There was a creak as the back door was opened slowly. A vague figure stood there, seemed to be peering out into the darkness.

Grimes remained perfectly still. He was well-hidden anyway, screened by the remains of an old privy and the sodden foliage of a mangy scrub of doubtful species.

The figure – it wasn't big enough to be Santos, passed along the back of the house and disappeared around the corner. There was the sound of movement round there. The figure did not appear again for some time but, when it did, it led two horses. Their hoofs made only a soft thud-thud on the ground, Grimes could barely hear it himself. He realized the beasts' hoofs had been muffled with burlap or something like that: an old owlhooter's trick.

The man left the horses at the small hitching rack and went back into the *cantina*, closing the door softly. The light still glowed thinly from the back window.

There was more waiting – while the horses stirred restlessly and Grimes was as taut as an overstrung fiddle-string.

Then the door opened again and a strange-shaped figure came through. Like a long mis-shapen animal. Grimes had to strain his eyes somewhat before he identified this strange creature as two men carrying a long bundle between them. One figure looked like the man Grimes had seen before. The other one was much bigger and couldn't be anyone else but Santos. And the bundle they carried between them . . . it looked suspiciously like a body.

When it was slung over the front of a saddle, with the smaller man mounted behind, it looked even more like a body.

Santos mounted the other horse and said something in a low voice. The two riders started off, the third rider lolling grotesquely.

The watching Grimes was in an agony of indecision. He wished he had brought a horse. Then he realized that, even if he had a horse, if he attempted to follow these two riders on a beast whose hoofs hadn't been 'muffled' he would be sure to be detected.

The two horsemen, travelling slowly, passed fairly close to him and almost immediately he ran towards the cantina. He paused for a moment at the door, then ran round the side of the place to the small stables. He was overjoyed when he discovered a spare horse there. He almost vaulted on to its back forthwith and set off after Santos and his pardner and their grisly burden. But he held on to himself and struck a match. Then he was glad he had had second thoughts. On the floor were strips of burlap and a coil of twine. Evidently Santos had had everything prepared: probably it wasn't the first time he had rode out on a 'muffled' cayuse. There was an old saddle hanging on the wall too.

The horse began to get a little skittish. Grimes gentled it with his hands, with his soothing voice. Then it was the work of moments for Grimes' nimble fingers to tie burlap strips round the four hoofs. He mounted the horse and urged him out of the stables.

The beast travelled smoothly and easily, despite the mufflers. Grimes didn't press him, knowing that the other mufflered horses wouldn't be going fast either, particularly as one of them had a double burden.

The rain was now only a faint drizzle and, to Grimes' regret, the sky was lightening, the moon striving to break through the leaden clouds.

Presently Grimes halted his horse and dismounted. He went down on his knees and pressed his ear to the wet ground. Slowly to him came the slow pulsating beat of hoofs. He was on the right track all right. Santos and his partner – and the 'silent' partner too – weren't far ahead.

They were moving into an arid area of scrub and boulders. Here a body could be thrown into a crevice or buried beneath a mound of stones and lost forever.

Grimes cursed as, slowly, the moon came out. The scene, bathed in the eerie watery light, was like something out of another world. He slowed his mount a little, glad that this beast he had borrowed was a surefooted one.

After a moment he dismounted again and pressed his ear to the ground. He couldn't hear anything now but the soughing of the wind. The other horses had stopped! Had Santos and his friend reached their destination or had they become aware that they were being tailed and were lying doggo, planning a bushwack parley?

Grimes took out his gun and hesitated. The rain had stopped completely. He reholstered the gun, mounted the horse again. Grimes, though he would not have called himself a brave man, was a very stubborn one. He went on.

He was on the prod as only a Westerner can be and not stopping to tot up his hand.

Lady Luck turned her back on him and the two horsemen, unencumbered, now rode at him out of the night. They started shooting and Grimes' gun was still entangled with his slicker when the first slug took him in his upper arm. He dropped the gun and almost left the saddle himself. His horse, scared by this sudden apparition from the night, turned tail and bolted.

Jolted on a sea of pain Grimes held on like grim death. He hardly felt the second slug which caught him in the back, paralysing him. His hands were glued to the reins. The horse was taking him home. But his pursuers, like avenging demons, were still at his heels.

He must get to the law; the only thought in his dazed mind was that he must get to the law!

The mufflers had been thrown from the horse's hoofs by the violence of his galloping. It was a nightmare ride but presently Grimes was aware that they were clattering down the main drag of Fishknife and that his pursuers were no longer behind him.

People, limmed against lighted windows, stared after the flying horseman. But Grimes wasn't aware of them – he must get to the law . . . get to the law. . . .

He managed to check the horse. He tumbled onto the sidewalk outside the sheriff's office. Pain clawed at him. Then the blackness threatened him again and he fought it. He was aware of somebody bending over him . . .

CHAPTER XIII

Johnny Rayno's men did their jobs well. Everything was perfectly timed. But to the men in the cabin it seemed that all hell had suddenly been let loose.

At the crash of the opened door a man went for his gun. Johnny's Colt bucked and flamed. The man yelled with pain, clutched his slug-burned arm. His gun remained in its holster.

There were levelled guns in front and behind them . . . and now the window was shattered and the face of Loopy Kenwood grinned like a demon's over yet another steady blue barrel.

Virg Craddock, white face taut, was in the front of the cabin party. Standing under the levelled guns of the law. Johnny Rayno, who carried a pair of Colts too, and had a rep almost as notorious as Virg's own. Virg was no fool. His pale eyes glowed hotly now but he kept his hands away from his two guns, figuring maybe his time would come.

He said, tonelessly, 'You can't kill us all.'

'Try us,' said Johnny laconically.

The bedroom door opened. 'Yes, try us,' said a feminine voice.

Mrs Maxwell and Prue stood there and they both held levelled guns.

'Good for you, maw,' said deputy-sheriff George Maxwell softly.

Jubel Maxwell glared at his wife and daughter and finally found his voice.

'Have all my family turned traitor?' His plea would have sounded ludicrous had it not been so impassioned. Prue answered for her mother and, no doubt, for George too. She talked sense.

'You're acting like a madman lately, dad. You seem determined to go out an' get yourself killed. Whether you realize it or not, none of us want that to happen to you. You're letting yourself be swayed by a bunch of selfish hotheads who've picked you for leader because they haven't the guts to fight their own battle. You've been hypnotised by Virg Craddock, hired killer, who has no stake in this business at all. He isn't your friend. He came here because you sent for him. But not as a friend – don't fool yourself, dad. His sort can smell easy pickings.'

She had finished and Virg Craddock was smiling mirthlessly, saying nothing. And even Jubel Maxwell was speechless too it seemed, overwhelmed by his daughter's unwonted eloquence.

'Good for you, sis,' said George softly and his mother's eyes were shining.

'You told the law,' Jubel burst out suddenly and he

was looking at his wife and daughter.

'How could we?' said Mrs. Maxwell. 'Neither of us have left the place, you know that. Besides, we didn't know what you were cooking up until a few minutes ago.'

'Don't make excuses to him, maw,' said George.

'I told the law,' said Harry the nester. 'I knew the Ace-High men didn't do the last raid. I told yuh that. Besides, don't you think they're ready for you any time you want to try anything? Ace-High is too old a fox to be caught napping.'

The men shuffled their feet. Some of them even began to look a mite sheepish. Expressions of baffled chagrin and temper chased each other across Jubel Maxwell's lantern-jawed visage. Virg Craddock was taut-faced, pale-eyed, sardonic.

The sheriff took over, turning to Darkie Boots, telling him to get their guns.

The coloured ranny moved neatly among the men, lifting their hardware, tossing it on to a convenient table.

The tension was almost unbelievable.

But, as yet, nobody had made a false move.

As Darkie approached Virg Craddock the latter's sardonic composure broke a little. 'I aim to keep my guns,' he said.

'You'll be treated the same as the rest,' said Johnny Rayno. The muzzles of his own guns tilted warily. Darkie neatly lifted Craddock's twin weapons and placed them with the rest. The Kansas gunfighter was frozen, his eyes glowed hotly now in a dead-white face.

Johnny Rayno's gaze swept the room. He said: 'There'll be no raiding tonight. You'll all go back home. You'll have your guns returned when I consider you're behaving yourselves nicely.

'No doubt,' he went on sardonically, anticipating inevitable rejoinders, 'you have other weapons at home with which to forestall any attack that may occur.'

Tonight seemed to be the night for fancy spouting. And, while Jubel Maxwell fumed and Virg Craddock was as watchful and deadly as a diamond-backed sidewinder, the sheriff went on. But his voice became suddenly different and Virg's head jerked up and the air of the room was suddenly full of pure murder. For the sheriff's words were now directed solely at the Kansas killer.

'You'll get out of this territory, my friend, and you won't come back.'

'I won't leave without my guns,' said Virg Craddock. There was no petulence about it; it was just a statement of fact.

Maybe the sheriff understood something of the man's feelings. They were strangely akin, these two, both gunfighters, both living by violence.

'So that's the way it is, is it?' said Johnny softly.

'Yes, that's the way it is,' said Virg Craddock. 'Maybe you'd like to take off your little tin star, sheriff, an' give me back my guns.'

'Don't let him ride yuh, Johnny,' burst out George Maxwell. 'We've got more important things to do right now than let ourselves be sidetracked by carrion. And you!' George glared at the Kansas gunman. 'Shut your trap or I'll get to work on yuh myself – an' I won't use guns. You need cuttin' down to size, pardner. If I'd had any sense I'd've thrown you out on your ear the first time I saw you. Give me half a chance an', by grab, I'll shore make up for lost time.'

'He means what he says, Virg,' said Jubel Maxwell suddenly, surprisingly. It might even have been possible to detect a ring of pride in Jubel's voice. Yessir, that was *his* boy.

Virg Craddock seemed unmoved by George's tirade. His pale eyes with their spots of flame were still fixed on the sheriff and he said:

'I'll be comin' to collect my guns sometime.'

For that moment it seemed that there were only these two men alone in the room.

'I'll be waiting,' said Johnny Rayno. 'Without my star.'

They understood each other now, these two. But to the other men watching and listening, unmoving, unspeaking, it seemed that something strange had happened and Mrs. Maxwell was seen to shiver as if she was cold.

'Let's get 'em out of here,' said George Maxwell harshly and the terrible spell was broken.

And, after that, it was easy – as men mounted their horses and rode away. Virg Craddock separated himself from the others and the night swallowed him up. Darkie Boots dumped all the guns in a burlap sack and tied it to his saddle-horn.

Jubel Maxwell was subdued. It was plain to see that his wife and daughter, probably for the first time they could remember, had the ascendancy. George volunteered to stay but his mother would not hear of it. He was a law-officer now and she was proud of him. He must carry on doing his duty. His father had nothing to say, did not try to dissuade George from the life he had chosen for himself.

The law party left the place. They paused on a rise to watch and listen in case any of the erstwhile raiding party still planned some kind of shennanigans. But the night was quiet.

Harry said: 'If you don't need us anymore, Jeb an' me will get back to our families.'

'Sure,' said Johnny. 'An' thanks for all your help. Will you be all right?'

'We'll be all right,' said Harry. 'We're all staying at my place for a while, seein' as it's a mite bigger than Jeb's.'

'D'yuh think any of your so-called friends will get spiteful an' try something because you turned on 'em?'

'Not them,' said Harry contemptuously. 'I know 'em. An' if that Virg Craddock shows up me an' Jeb'll cut him down an' bury him for yuh.'

'Sure thing,' said the taciturn Jeb.

Then the two men sang out their 'goodnights' and left.

'You never can tell about people can yuh?' said George Maxwell cryptically.

They rode on towards town. George, Darkie, Johnny.

Loopy Kenwood too, riding with real men now, matching them in stature and proud of the fact.

As they rode into the main drag of Fishknife, they sensed trouble right away. Men were out on the boardwalks, gesticulating in the yellow light, peering down the street.

The law-party set their horses faster and as they got further on, saw other men hurrying towards the sheriff's office, saw the crumpled bundle on the boardwalk there, the man bending over it.

They reached the office before anybody else, left their horses. The bending man was a respectable little storekeeper Johnny knew well by sight. The man looked up, said shakily, 'It's Grimes, the livery-man. He's been shot bad.'

Johnny went down on one knee beside the wounded man. The others spread out, ready to keep the approaching sightseers at bay.

'He fell off his horse here,' babbled the little storekeeper. 'I didn't hear any shots or see anybody.'

Grimes was still alive but Johnny could see he was a goner. Shot to ribbons. The man's eyes blazed for a moment, his mouth worked. He got one word out. A name. *Santos*! Then he died.

Johnny straightened up, thinking fast. He turned on the little storekeeper. 'Did you hear what he said?'

'Yes, I heard it. He said . . .'

'That's enough. Keep your mouth shut. Understand?'

'I understand, suh. Sure – sure.'

Like underfed vultures who had smelled blood, the undertaker and his assistant were suddenly on the scene. They took the body away. The craning, peering folks began to disperse. Away from death, back to the brittle lights.

Johnny had orders for Loopy and Darkie. They were to circulate, drop the news that Grimes had died without speaking, that there was no clue as to who had killed him.

Doc Jupp suddenly put in an appearance. Mayor Prom Varney had come out of his coma and was talking. He wanted to see the sheriff right away.

Johnny weighed things up, said he'd come. George Maxwell volunteered to watch the Santos *cantina*. He gave his assurance that he would keep out of sight and wouldn't try a play until Johnny turned up.

They separated, Johnny going with the little doctor.

Prom Varney was propped up in bed. He was even smiling in a vinegary kind of way. It was obvious that Fishknife's lawyer-mayor was tougher than he looked. He told the sheriff that he had remembered something. Before he was beaten unconscious he had heard a name mentioned. The name of who was probably the leader of his attackers. A bloodthirsty individual who had suggested stringing Varney up. A man called 'Virg'.

Johnny Rayno cursed. Parts of the puzzle were beginning to fall into place. He wished now that he had held Virg Craddock when he had the chance. He realized that it was only his own vain pride that had enabled him to let the Kansas gunfighter ride away, made him believe the man's promise to come back, meet Johnny alone, just the two of them and no lawman's star to tip the scales.

Would Craddock come back for his guns like he had promised? A man who was the subject of bloody legend might do just that, hoping to add another scalp to his belt, another notch to his gun, another legend to the bloodstained saga.

Would Craddock be able to do that, Johnny wondered. He was fast himself, could Craddock be faster? Legend said he could. Legend would have it that Craddock could take Johnny and go on. To more killings, more depredations.

Craddock might come back, might kill Johnny. Either way he was loose. Should not Johnny, as a lawman, have taken Craddock into custody when he had the chance? In letting Craddock go had he not acted with a queer inverted idealism, a following-through of the code of the gun fighter? If, through doing this, he ultimately lost his own skin; well, he would only have got what he asked for.

But other people might suffer too; with Craddock free once more, other folks would inevitably suffer. And that would be Johnny's fault because, despite his high-falutin' pronouncement to Ace-High Logan, he had, when the test came, acted like a swaggering *cabellero* instead of a sober lawman.

He cursed again, aware then that Lawyer Varney was still babbling.

'Speak, man. Do you know this Virg?'

'Yes, I know him.'

'Then as Mayor of this town I order you to get him.'

There was a queer dignity about the little man with the bandaged head sitting up there against his mound of pillows.

'I'll get him,' said Johnny Rayno and he left the room.

CHAPTER XIV

It was raining again. The main drag was a river of mud, ballasted by duckboards, burlap sacking and ashes. But still men sank up to their ankles in the viscid black stuff and horses floundered, wagons got bogged down. Johnny kept to the boardwalks as much as possible. His thoughts were as black as the mud, as melancholy as the lowering skies and driving rain.

A wagon and two horses were caught in the mire opposite the Santos *cantina*. Two men, plastered in mud, were heaving and straining, making the air even thicker with their curses.

Johnny skirted the melee, made his way gingerly to the opposite sidewalk. High-heeled riding-boots were not particularly ideal for walking, even under the best conditions; but right now they were hopeless, getting more clogged-up and heavier with every step. Johnny wished he had brought his horse.

Maybe he would need a horse, at that. . . . If Santos made a break for it. . . .

A figure detached itself suddenly from the shadows

in front of him and he forgot his horse. But this was only George Maxwell, the man Johnny had come to meet. And George spoke fast.

'Santos came down to the bar a few minutes ago. I saw him through the window. He spoke to a couple of men then went out through the door behind the bar. I thought maybe he meant to light out so I've bin round back. He ain't come out. There's a light in one of the upper windows back there so maybe Santos is upstairs. There are three horses in the little stables out there. Two of 'em are still saddled an' they look as if they have been ridden hard quite recently.'

'Good work, pardner,' said the sheriff.

He paused for a moment then went on: 'I'm going round back. I'm going in that way. I aim to take Santos quietly and alive if possible. I want you to stay here an' watch the front in case he tries to make a break this way, hoping to cover himself.' Johnny waved a hand, encompassing the mud, the bogged-down wagon, the cursing teamsters, the men who stood now on the sidelines and bawled ribald encouragement. 'If Santos comes out, clip him. If he goes for his gun shoot him. But try not to kill him – I want him to talk.'

George nodded, loosened his gun in its holster beneath his dripping slicker. Johnny, clad in a plaid blanket-coat, was glad his own guns were dry too. He went on round the side of the cantina and reached the yard. He looked up. A light shone in the middle window upstairs.

There were two windows downstairs, dark, a door in

between them. Johnny tried the door. It would not budge. He tried both windows. They were fastened tightly too. He took out his gun, swung it sharply, smashed a pane with the steel barrel. He waited, listening. There was no sound but the soughing of the wind and the steady muffled beat of the rain. He put his hand through the gap, found the catch and lifted it, opened the window. He listened some more, then, after a moment, climbed through.

He stood for a moment, allowing his eyes to get accustomed to the darkness. There was no sound. The storm was muffled. By the stale smells that rose to Johnny's nostrils he judged this was a kitchen. He saw a sink; then he spotted a door and crossed to it. It opened at his touch and he passed through into a passage. Light shone dimly on a flight of stairs. There was a lantern up there someplace. Johnny climbed the stairs. The light got brighter.

He reached the landing. He found the lantern, unhooked it and blew out the light. A yellow beam still filtered from beneath a door in front of him. He drew a gun. He crossed to the door and flung it open.

With his back to the door, Santos had been packing a large portmanteau which lay on the bed before him. Evidently he hadn't meant to take any chances on whether Grimes talked or not. He whirled, hand dipping to his gun.

'Hold it!' rapped Johnny.

Santos froze, one large hand clawlike, the other resting on the edge of the portmanteau.

'What ees the meaning of thees?' he demanded.

His accent was more evident than usual, giving away the fact of his surprise and nervousness. His fleshily-handsome face was flushed, his pomaded ringlets in disarray. Even his little moustache seemed bedraggled.

Nevertheless, standing upright now, he bulked largely, powerfully, in the small room. He seemed to dwarf Johnny. The nostrils of his hawklike nose flared. His eyes glared at Johnny; but there was a shifty look in them too.

'Going someplace, Santos?' said the sheriff.

The big handsome Mexican grinned. But there was no mirth there. He had his voice under control too, when he answered. 'A business trip. One – two days. If it is any thing to do with you. I ask you again: what is the meaning of this?'

'You're not goin' anyplace, *amigo*,' said Johnny. 'I'm arresting you for the murder of Grimes, the hostler.'

The man's eyes flickered. He grinned again. 'You must be loco,' he boomed.

'I ain't got time to argue,' said Johnny. 'I'm takin' you to the jail right now. Turn around.'

Fury flamed momentarily in the Mexican's eyes. 'I'll make you pay for this,' he said. He turned slowly.

Johnny went closer, lifted the man's gun. Santos moved again then; it seemed incredible that such a heavy man could be so fast. His fingers dipped into the open portmanteau before him; a shirt swung in his hand, wrapped itself around the sheriff's face.

Santos' own gun went off in Johnny's hand. The slug ploughed into the ceiling. Johnny dropped the gun and clawed at the clinging thing which obscured his sight. A blow caught him on the shoulder and he staggered backwards. The shirt fell to the floor but, before Johnny could raise his own gun – remembering even in this desperate moment that he wouldn't kill Santos if he could help it – the gun was swept from his hand.

Johnny closed with the big man, forgetting all weapons now.

Santos got him in a bearlike hug and Johnny wished he hadn't been so precepitate. Those fat arms felt like bands of hot steel. He fought for a breathing-space, working both fists like pistons, sinking them into the big man's vulnerable stomach. Santos grunted horribly, belching hot breath into Johnny's face. His grasp began to slacken.

Johnny pushed with all his strength and Santos staggered away from him. Johnny went after him, swung a left, a right, feeling them connect. Santos' dark face became stained with blood. Then Santos covered up, breathing heavily as fleshy men do, but still very dangerous, very fast. He slid out of Johnny's way, swung a foot. Johnny almost ran into the crippling jab. The toe of Santos' boot grazed his shin. Goaded, Johnny flung a blow at him and missed. Santos retaliated and only thumped his opponent's shoulder.

Next moment, however, they were swinging punches like maniacs, not using any finesse now; slogging. Santos began to give ground, wearying now, trying to find an opening and get to close quarters again. But Johnny was wary now. He used his long arms, his fists like hammers at the end of them, keeping the big man at bay, cutting him gradually, cruelly down to size.

Santos got a blow in from time to time but, despite his bulk, he was hopelessly outclassed. If he could get close he could break every bone in this dancing monkey's body. But he couldn't get close, those fists like whips kept him at bay. Here was a man who knew the bare-knuckle game and seemed to be determined to cut his opponent scientifically to ribbons . . .

Santos was half-blinded by his own blood. He began to back . . . back . . . his big flabby hands waving like paws in front of him. A fist driven into his middle doubled him up. Another descended like a hammer in the back of his neck. The floor came up to meet him, exploded in his face. Momentarily, he blacked out.

When awareness returned to him he tried to get up. The hammer descended on him once more, bringing blinding pain. He went down again. As if sifted through layers of wool the sheriff's voice came through to him.

'I don't see why I should bust my hands on you. From now on I aim to use the barrel of my gun. Have you ever seen a man pistol-whipped until his flesh was stripped from his bones, Santos? You'd better start talking unless you want to die slowly.'

'I am finished. What ees eet you want to know?'

'You killed Grimes didn't you?'

'Yes, I killed heem. He was a meddling fool.'

'He knew you had killed Pedro. Why did you kill Pedro – because he knew too much?'

'Yes. He had ridden with us once or twice. After you asked him questions he started to ask me for money. I knew that if I didn't keep giving him money for clothes and whiskey he would tell you all he knew. So I killed heem.'

Santos wormed his way upwards until his back was resting against the edge of the bed. He blinked up at Johnny, at the gun in Johnny's hand. The handsome florid Mexican big-shot was now a sorry sight.

'All right,' said the sheriff. 'Let's have the whole story. You run a gang don't you? You're behind the raiding that's been going on lately.'

'Not me alone,' said Santos hotly. 'Virg Craddock too. I knew him from way back. When he got here, he approached me. He figured if we started a range-war there'd be easy pickings. We used Jubel Maxwell, playing him and his friends against Ace-High Logan. We ran off nester stock, knowing the nesters would blame Logan. We aimed to run off Logan stock too, prime stock. We've got markets.'

'A pretty scheme,' said Johnny. 'Where's the hideout?'

'In the hills. Back of the big rock they call The Jackass.'

'All right, *amigo*. Get up.'

Santos pressed his hands on the floor beside him. He began to lever himself upwards. His feet shot out, catching Johnny below the knees. Johnny was knocked off balance. Vainly he tried to save himself. He hit the floor with his back, with a force that knocked all the breath from him. He managed to hold onto the gun. He realized with chagrin that Santos, despite his looks, hadn't been as badly beaten as he'd pretended. His willingness to talk had given him time to get some of his strength back – to think, to act.

Johnny rolled over. The door slammed behind Santos. The key grated into the lock.

Johnny flung himself at the door.

It was locked all right!

He pointed his gun at the lock, pressed the trigger. The shot boomed deafeningly in the enclosed place. Blue smoke drifted; the door swung open. Johnny ran into the passage. He could hear Santos' bootheels clattering on the stairs.

Johnny went down the stairs two at a time, strange stairs: at the bottom he almost lost his footing. Santos was halfway across the *cantina*. Men were breaking away each side of him, getting out of the way of his bull-like charge. Santos was yelling.

The doors closed behind him and another man stood in his place. A flashily-dressed Mexican with levelled gun. His first shot dug into the stair-rail at Johnny's side.

Johnny paused, raised his own gun, levelled it coolly. Here was a wild man, a shooting fool. His second shot missed completely, too. There was nothing between the two of them but space. Johnny thumbed the hammer of his gun twice.

The Mexican took both slugs in the chest. They

knocked him backwards into the doors. He slid to the foot of them and lay still.

Johnny had both guns out now. He moved like a cat as he crossed the floor, springily, warily. A gunfighter on a hair-trigger, but cool.

Nobody moved.

Then from outside, in the night, came a hideous blatter of shots and Johnny covered the rest of the distance at a run. He went through the door, spun sideways into the shadows, wary of shots from in front, or behind.

'It's all right, Johnny,' a voice yelled.

George Maxwell stood over the still bulk of a man lying face-downwards in the mud. Johnny joined him. George turned the body over with the toe of his boot. Even through the mud and the blood the once-handsome features of Santos were still recognizable.

'Sorry I had to kill him, chief,' said George. 'But it was him or me.'

'Forget it,' said Johnny. 'I found out what I wanted to know anyway. Wait a minute.' He turned, strode back to the cantina.

Dark faces receded before him. He bent over the man on the floor. Santos' flashily-dressed pardner was quite dead and Johnny was able to check up on something that had, only momentarily, caught his eye.

The man's Spanish-style pipestem trousers were decorated by plugged *pesos*. On the left leg one of the silver coins was missing. Johnny delved into a pocket and brought forth the *peso* he had found out on the range. It matched all right. He was satisfied. He left the body there and went back to George, who, his hand on his gun was ignoring questions, keeping sightseers at bay.

'Do you know a rock in the hills called The Jackass?'

'Sure. It's shaped like a jackass's head, big ears an' all.'

'Virg Craddock an' the gang are up there. They're just a bunch of rustlers an' looters. Virg has been using your dad and rest of the nesters as catspaw.'

'Dad'll have to know about this.'

'That's what I thought . . .' Johnny paused as Darkie Boots and Loopy Kenwood appeared.

'Here, Loopy, go get some hosses, pronto.'

'Sure thing.' Loopy scuttled away.

'We'll ride,' said Johnny. 'George, you an' Loopy go see your dad, tell him the story, tell him to get as many of the nesters together that he can. Darkie an' me will go to the Ace-High and get some men from there. If you see Virg Craddock shoot him on sight. I had hoped to have that pleasure myself, but still, we wouldn't want him to warn the others. We'll all meet at your dad's place in about an hour and a half.'

Loopy arrived with the horses. The four men mounted, left town, the gaping townsfolk, the dead hulk in the mud beneath the driving rain.

CHAPTER XV

The ranch was in darkness but as Darkie and Johnny clattered their horses past the corral, lights flashed in the bunkhouse window.

Rafe Dawson came out, clad in vest and pants, but still in his stockinged feet. The inevitable sawn-off shotgun was cradled in his arm, the muzzle pointed outwards. Other men came out behind him. Guns bristled.

'Stand easy, you skittish critturs,' bawled Darkie Boots. Johnny said to him, 'Tell Rafe what's going on. Liven the boys up. I'll go see the Old Man.'

They separated. Johnny dismounted at the back door of the ranch house, clattered on to the verandah. The door opened. Amy stood there, a rifle in her hands.

'Take it easy, honey.'

'Johnny Rayno ! What a time to come a-calling.' Then her voice became grave. 'What's happened?'

'We've found out whose behind the raiding and burning. The nesters had nothing to do with it. Your dad'll have to know. I guess he'll want to ride too.'

'I guess he will.' She seemed very small in the darkness. He pressed her arm and went on, knowing his way well now, even in the darkness.

Ace-High met him in the lighted hallway. The old man stood in shirt and trousers, a gun in his hand. Johnny talked fast. When he had finished the old man said:

'Go on back. I'll get dressed properly then I'll be right with you.'

'Yes, suh.'

Johnny went back into the kitchen, where Amy had lighted the lamp. She was clad in a brilliant intricately-woven Indian robe and had Indian moccasins on her feet. Under the light her hair shone like ripe corn. She was a strangely bewitching picture. She came to Johnny, her eyes enormous. He took her in his arms.

'He's going?' she said.

'What did you think?'

'I know.' Her voice was muffled against his chest. 'I won't say I'm not scared because I am, scared for both of you.'

'Don't worry, we'll be back before you can spit.'

'Johnny Rayno!'

He chuckled. He caught hold of her chin and lifted her face. 'Give me one of those beautiful smiles of yours.'

She smiled, her eyes shining. 'All right, you big ape. Now kiss me.'

He kissed her well; until a gruff cough from the doorway broke them apart in confusion.

'Bless you, my chillun,' said Ace-High with an old-devilish grin.

Johnny followed him out to the verandah. Then they turned.

The girl stood in the doorway. 'I want you both back in one piece,' she said.

The two men exchanged glances. 'That's the way it's gonna be,' said Ace-High. 'Or I'll want to know the reason why.'

'Go with God,' said the girl softly.

They echoed the old Spanish farewell.

The men were waiting. A horse was ready and saddled for Ace-High. The rain had stopped and now, as they started out, the moon came from behind the clouds.

'Aw, hell,' said Rafe Dawson.

'Never mind,' said Ace-High. 'We'll be able to see to shoot straight.'

It was a bigger party that, not so long later, left Jubel Maxwell's little spread. Jubel himself rode side by side with his old enemy, Ace-High Logan. George and Johnny, right behind them, couldn't help exchanging congratulatory glances. George said none of them had seen hide nor hair of Virg Craddock. Maybe the Kansas gunslinger was at the hideout with the rest of the bunch, unless he had left the territory altogether.

The rock outcrop called The Jackass bulked grotesquely in the silvery moonlight. Men had long since divested themselves of their slickers or coats and rode unencumbered, their hands not too far away from their guns. They stared upwards at the fantastic rock head with the long snout and mule-like ears. They climbed now, the horses finding it hard going on the rocky uneven surface.

They reached a smaller outcrop, semi-circular like a miniature barricade. Then Ace-High Logan took command and nobody gainsaid him.

'We'll leave the horses here,' he said. 'It'll be easier on foot, and not so durned noisy either.'

They dismounted. They fanned out a little as they began to climb, using cover as much as possible in case they had already been spotted. Johnny, George, Jubel, Ace-High, Rafe, Loopy, Darkie, Harry, Jeb ... and many others.

Men looked at each other, walking like cats. The moonlight was brilliant and men cursed it. They did not bunch now but kept apart as much as possible. But still they were good targets for anyone who might be waiting up there, waiting until he saw the whites of their eyes.

The shadows up there were black and could hide countless things. But the rocks were washed white and brilliant and men's faces white, their eyes like black watchful caverns, but pinpoints of light showing in them as they moved them nervously, looking about them and upwards, their hands on their guns.

The going was rough and it was well that they had left their horses. Stones rattled beneath their feet and now and then a man slipped, cursed softly, deep in his throat.

They reached the big outcrop called The Jackass and began to skirt it on both sides. Then there were soft exclamations and most of them stopped to look, holding up those behind them.

Many of them knew what lay behind The Jackass, had seen this little pocket in the hills, this valley before. But none of them before had seen it full of livestock. It was cattle mostly. There wasn't such a heck of a lot of it really but it looked a lot in that enclosed space.

'This is it all right,' said one man.

Another man cried out suddenly in agony. His white face was thrown back, blood gushed blackly in the moonlight. Another man caught him but he was already dead. The whiplash echoes of a rifle died away in the stillness, then broke loose again.

There was only one man down there, a lookout. A marksman too. Johnny Rayno's hat was whipped from his head by another slug. He went down on one knee, lost his balance on the uneven ground and rolled. His body was bumped and jarred and scratched. Half-winded, he came to rest finally against a boulder. He was in cover once more anyway. He flexed his limbs. No great harm done.

Men were moving down behind him, dodging from cover to cover. Gun ready, Johnny peeped over the top of his rock. He saw the man climbing the slope at the other side of the valley. Gunfire rolled behind him. He raised his own weapon, drew a bead on the frantically-scrabbling figure. A rifle spoke behind him. The figure became like a jointless puppet; it rolled back down the slope, came to rest, lay still.

'Keep goin',' barked Ace-High Logan. 'Make it fast – but don't get too close together.'

Johnny rose, found himself limping. Men were moving all around him. Some of them passed him. Darkie Boots reached his side. 'You all right, Johnny?'

'Sure. Just a knock.' Then they were separated again. Most of them were halfway up the opposite slope when the shooting started once more. But they had the bits between their teeth now and they kept on. A man gave a womanish cry and collapsed with a smashed knee-cap. A friend stayed behind with him. The rest, scurrying and dodging like black ants in the moonlight, kept on.

A man clutched at his stomach, staggered forward a few more steps then crumpled up. He began to roll then, moaning, horribly. Two other men caught him but by that time he was silent and they left him there.

Then the first line of them were over the top and the defenders were retreating before them.

There were a couple of rickety frame cabins, temporary structures, on that tiny mesa. The defenders took cover in or among them, but, like those structures, the cover was flimsy. Like trained soldiers, many of them acting as if they had done this all their lives the attacking force kept on. They dodged from cover to cover like seasoned skirmishers. Two nesters had been killed. Their comrades were like avenging demons. The shooting from the defenders was wilder, they were becoming demoralized. They were border desperadoes, Mexicans and half-breeds; they broke; cut and run.

Many of them were dropped in their tracks. One ran in the wrong direction, ran like a chicken with no head, towards the guns, screaming for mercy in a mixture of bastardized Spanish and Apache.

He was fetched down with a bullet in his leg. Johnny Rayno reached him.

'The gringo, Virg Craddock: where is he?'

The half-breed saw death in the lifted gun, the eyes dark in the moonlight, with pinpoints of fury in their depths.

The man's own eyes rolled in his dark face. 'He ees in the small cabin, *señore*. Plees. He has the iron stove against the window for protection. Plees. . . .'

Johnny realized the fury had died. Captives were being rounded up. Others lay dead or wounded. Men were coming out of cover, walking towards the cabins. Was Virg Craddock finished too, Johnny wondered . . .

Then a gun cracked from the smaller cabin and a man staggered, clutching his shoulder and Johnny knew Virg was still alive.

'Down, you fools,' bellowed Ace-High Logan and men fell flat again.

Johnny crawled over to the old man, spoke fast. Ace-High seemed to be demurring; he shook his leonine head. George Maxwell wriggled closer and joined him. Another man showed too much head and almost had his scalp blown off as the gun cracked once more in the cabin. The echoes died away and there was comparative silence again. Then, above the faint soughing of the wind, a voice rose clearly.

'Virg Craddock, is that you? This is Johnny Rayno. Are you listening?'

'I'm listening, sheriff.' The sardonic voice was muffled a little, but clear.

'I made you a promise. I aim to keep that promise. Do you remember the promise I made?'

'Yes, I remember it, sheriff.' The voice was more sardonic than ever.

'I'm taking off my badge and I'm handing it to Ace-High Logan.' Johnny suited the action to the words. Ace-High took the silver star and said nothing.

'Step out with your guns holstered and I'll come to meet you. If you kill me you'll be given a chance to get away. You have the word of Ace-High Logan for that.'

The Old Man's own voice rose now. 'You hear that, all of you. I'm going along with it.'

There was dead silence for a moment; then cries of assent. Then Johnny Rayno's voice rang out again.

'Are you coming out, Virg?'

Johnny knew his man and had a strange respect for him; knew what his answer would be and it came.

'I'm coming out, Johnny.'

There was silence again. The men waited. Then, as Johnny Rayno rose, the figure appeared in the cabin door.

Johnny began to walk, limping a little. Virg Craddock came forward to meet him, hands swinging at his sides.

The scene was set in the pale pitiless moonlight.

There was no sound except the soughing of the wind and the faint tap-tap of the men's feet over the rocks.

And then the tapping stopped and there was only the wind like a dirge.

The blatter of gunfire was hideous, for both men had drawn and shot; and the echoes rolled away and the silence fell again except for a tiny gasping sound which was like part of the wind.

One of the men was on the ground but was trying to rise, gasping as he tried. But it was too much for him and life left him and he lay still, a small bundle in the moonlight.

Johnny Rayno looked at the torn sleeve of his shirt and the red bullet-gash beneath it, black in the moonlight. He looked for a moment at the still form before him.

He turned slowly and walked back to where Ace-High Logan and the rest of his friends awaited him.

'Let's go home, son,' said the Old Man softly.